Monty The Magnificat

Tina Haydamacha

Published by Tina Haydamacha, 2022.

MONTY THE MAGNIFICAT

First edition. February 11, 2022.

Copyright © 2022 Tina Haydamacha.

ISBN: 979-8201674892

Written by Tina Haydamacha.

Table of Contents

You guided the stroke of my pen throughout my life and introduced me to a creative world with infinite possibilities. I wish you were here. Thanks Mom!

Chapter 1

MICHAEL PAIGE, AN ARCHITECT in lower Manhattan was in his office putting the finishing touches on a construction project when he noticed a manila folder being slipped under his door. Inside the folder, he found a newspaper clipping describing how commercial developers were about to buy out a fleet of ships in Black Sails Bay that dated back as far as the seventeenth century.

As he stared at photographs of the old ships about to be scrapped for profit, stories he had read as a child came rushing back to him. One summer vacation he became particularly fascinated with a Reader's Digest story about Black Sails Bay off the Carolina Coast and the renegade pirates known to anchor their ships there.

The folklore about mysterious voodoo rituals surrounding the harbor attracted sailors who dabbled in black magic and often wrought havoc among the colonists.

Rumor had it that pirates would hide their treasure around the bay, because they believed the spells cast by a powerful sorceress would protect it.

The lure of the Atlantic Seaboard that once played host to pirates reignited Michael's passion to explore the bay. He was convinced that the article was a sign that Black Sails Bay held the key to something more, and he wanted to find the answers.

His wife of eleven years welcomed the idea of raising her family in a town shrouded in mystery. After all, Monica had been born in Colonial Massachusetts and grew up listening to the infamous story of the Salem Witch Trials that took place back in 1692. At the tender age of fifteen, Monica was so fascinated by the people accused of witchcraft that she entered the annual art contest for Salem Town's local newspaper. She won first place for her charcoal sketch of Tituba, one of the first women to be accused of practicing witchcraft.

This moment defined her fascination with the arts and lead her to pursue a career in art history at Brooklyn College, where she met and married Michael Paige and subsequently had two children. Timmy, who just celebrated his ninth birthday, was small for his age but made up for it with his huge imagination. His little sister, Jackie, who would be four years old next spring, was a budding actress who would break into song at a moment's notice.

THIS FAMILY DYNAMIC of creativity overflowed into a shared interest and fascination with art objects that had shaped the past and led to the exciting world of scavenger hunting for the whole Paige family. The occasional weekend family ritual would take place at their nearby park or else in their spacious loft apartment, where they would search for hidden vintage items carefully selected from their personal library.

Scavenger hunting became an important family event and a way for Michael and Monica to share their love of history with their children. It didn't take long for Michael to realize his children couldn't resist the game, which prompted him to pitch the idea of relocating to a town whose pirate past could mean treasures left behind long ago. The perfect place to escape the hustle and bustle of big city life was about to become the key that would unlock doors to century-old secrets.

The Paige family set off on their long journey well prepared with sing-a-longs, word games, and places to stop for picnics along the way. But after hours and hours of driving, exhaustion began to take a toll on everyone. Michael took the next exit into Harrisonburg, which was seven miles from the exact midpoint of Mount Crawford Virginia.

The trip felt like an eternity to the children who were cooped up in the back seat of the station wagon with moving boxes and bags of clothing piled up to the roof. The nearby sandwich shop was a comforting sight to everyone as they pulled in to restock their food supply for the final leg of the journey.

As Monica took the children to wash up, she passed a crowd of travelers hovering around a television set in the back of the shop. The National Weather Service had interrupted the regular scheduled program to alert the public to the arrival of a storm off the coast of Carolina that was due to land the following day. Soon after, Michael returned with the Paige family favorite, a bubbling hot pizza with extra cheese, which brought cheers of delight from the tired children. "We'll be there before the storm hits," Michael remarked as he watched the children gobble up their pizza.

"That's a relief." Monica looked up and smiled as she packed up the extra snacks to take in the car.

"All the same, we better get moving. It's going to get dark soon." Michael added.

An hour into the trip, an emergency weather update interrupted Monica's favorite country station. The storm had moved in faster than predicted and was going to make landfall along the South Carolina Coast on the very day they were to move into their new home.

"We'll have to drive straight through if we want to beat the storm." Michael's voice held a note of urgency.

"Thank goodness the children fell asleep before the alert came over the radio," Monica replied.

She rummaged in the glove compartment for the road map in the hope of finding shelter as they drove into the path of the storm. Unfortunately, they'd passed the last of the rest stops miles before, and there was no turning back.

The next few hours became a traveler's worst nightmare as Michael struggled to drive through the powerful gusting winds. Lightning suddenly cracking its whip across the sky woke the children. Jackie let out a scream so loud Timmy covered his ears. She grabbed her Hello Kitty blanket and was hiding underneath it just as the sound of rolling thunder boomed overhead. The storm was taking its toll on the old station wagon as it swerved along the muddy road. A firm grip on the steering wheel was the best Michael could do to hold the car steady against the wild winds that tried to throw it off course.

"We're heading right into the storm," Michael said. He glanced anxiously at Monica.

"How old do you think those trees are?" Monica wondered, staring at the limbs thrashing in the wind.

"Well, they look as though they have been here for hundreds of years," he replied.

"Maybe there are superheroes hiding in the forest," Timmy blurted out excitedly.

"You're silly," said Jackie as she peeked out under her blanket.

"Not as silly as you," he said tickling his baby sister.

Unexpectedly, the windshield wiper froze making it difficult for Michael to see as he desperately tried to find the entrance to their new home. He pictured the three-story, Southern-style mansion with eight rooms and a servants' quarter dating back to the 1500s and standing on 800 acres of land overlooking the Carolina Coast. Flowering dogwoods, blackjack oak, and sassafras were among the many beautiful trees that surrounded the historical home.

He squinted through the windshield. Ah! There was the turn. But just as he was about to make the turn, an enormous bolt of lightning came crashing through the trees, forcing him to jam on the brakes. It was eerily silent for just a few moments as they all took a deep breath, until an ominous cracking sound could be heard directly above their heads.

"Hold on tight," Michael said as he threw the car into reverse and pressed hard on the gas. Within seconds, a huge tree branch broke off and crashed to the road, missing the car by only a few inches.

"Are you up for a challenge, son?"

"What do you mean, Dad?"

"I need your help moving the branch out of the way."

"This is so cool."

"Hurry! The rain is coming down hard," said Michael.

Jackie scrambled over the front seat and snuggled in closer to her mother. "Mommy, I'm scared."

"Don't worry, honey. Everything will be all right."

Timmy was able to lift the lighter, narrower end of the branch while his father grabbed the heavier end. They pushed the branch away from the front of the car, but not before they were soaked clear down to the bone.

"Get into the car son. We have to move fast," Michael shouted.

Jackie quickly crawled into the back seat as her brother jumped in next to her.

"I'm freezing," he said as he sat shivering from his soaking wet clothes.

"You can share my blanket," she uttered as she tucked it under his chin.

Monica moved closer to her husband and held on to his arm as he drove over the broken branches that littered the road ahead. As he tried to straddle the gullies in the road, the car began to tilt to one side.

"Look Out! We're going to tip over," Timmy shouted.

"Hold on tight, everybody," Michael said urgently.

Jackie tumbled down onto the floor of the car, bouncing around with every turn until the road began to smooth out and the car was finally clear of danger.

"Mommy, Mommy!" Jackie sounded as though she was going to cry.

"Everything is all right now, sweetheart," Monica said, turning to look down at her.

Timmy began to conjure up ideas for his first adventure as he gazed deep into the forest. Often, his wild imagination brought him into a world of make believe where villains and goblins ruled the world.

"Do you think we will ever meet a real pirate dad? Timmy asked.

"Pirates lived in this town in the 1700's and could be related to some of the townspeople here," Michael added.

"Wow! That would be awesome," said Timmy as he leaned down to pull Jackie up on to the seat.

"Ok everybody. Just a little bit longer said Monica as she gathered her belongings.

Suddenly, another gaping hole appeared in the road forcing Michael to swerve the station wagon one last time away from danger. Shortly after, a sigh of relief came over everyone as the difficult journey finally came to an end.

Chapter 2

AT LONG LAST, THE TIRING drive was over and there through the trees stood the biggest house Timmy and Jackie had ever seen. On the count of three, everyone grabbed something from the car and dashed for the house. Monica pulled out a large can of soup and a block of American cheese from the travel cooler and set it on the kitchen table. A steaming hot bowl of tomato soup with a grilled cheese sandwich seemed to save the day for everyone.

"My mother used to make this for me every time a storm passed through our neighborhood. I always felt so warm inside with every bite," Michael commented.

"Yummy, I love grilled cheese," Jackie said, as she sat, still shivering from the storm.

"Let's go see what's upstairs after we eat," Timmy added.

As soon as the two children had finished their soup, they bolted up the stairs to embark on their very own version of a scavenger hunt for hidden treasures.

"What's in that room?" Jackie curiously asked.

The sense of adventure was so exciting that she forgot all about being scared and ran ahead down the long dark hallway. She climbed onto a wooden step stool that sat outside the old rickety door and stretched as far as she could to reach the doorknob. As she leaned into the door, it slowly opened as if someone from the other side were giving her a hand. She squeezed her pint-size body through the opening and discovered an old wooden chest in the far corner of the room.

"Look what I found," she shouted to her brother as she struggled to open the lid to the old chest.

"Ok, Jackie. You grab this end and pull up with all your might."

But Jackie's big smile turned into a pout as she looked down at the pile of dirty old rags left behind by the previous owners.

"Wait! What's that sticking out?" her brother said as he pulled some of the rags from the trunk.

Jackie reached her little hands deep down into the bundle of rags and squealed with delight when she pulled out a beautiful doll with tattered clothing. She didn't waste any time hugging her new doll and rushed out of the room so fast she ran straight into her mother's arms.

"Look what I found, Mommy. Can I keep her? Can I keep her please, please, please?"

"Of course, you can, sweetheart. Why don't you take her with you to bed tonight?"

"Oh boy! I just love her and she's all mine." Jackie hopped and skipped down the hall, beaming.

Timmy was still busy pulling everything out of the wooden chest onto the floor until he noticed a small brown leather pouch inside a pair of old slippers. He desperately tried to open the pouch, but the leather straps were tied together too tightly.

"Dad! Dad!" he yelled as he rushed down the stairs and into the kitchen.

"What an old pouch. Grab me a knife out of the drawer, son."

The tip of a carving knife did the trick as Michael twisted the drawstring just enough to open the pouch. Inside was an old piece of silk cloth that was wrapped around a rusted old metal object.

"What is it, Dad?"

"You found a very old compass that was used by ship captains long, long ago."

"Wow! How does it work?"

"Well, the magnetized pointer that is set to the north heading will move freely according to the Earth's magnetic field."

"Oh boy! But, uh, what does all that mean?"

Michael glanced out of the window. "Well, the rain has slowed down a bit, so grab your raincoat and come outside. Don't forget the compass. Now, I want you to stand by the large blackjack oak tree down by the entrance to the house."

Timmy jumped over every puddle he could find as he made his way to the old oak tree.

"Now, aim the compass at the house while keeping your elbows by your side, and tell me what it reads," his father shouted.

"Wow! It's pointing to the letter N, but what does that mean again?"

"It means our house is on the north side. Let's get back inside, Timmy. There's still a lot of work to be done before nightfall. We can take another look at the compass tomorrow."

Once inside, Michael stacked some logs inside the fireplace and prepared to get the chill out of the house before they all turned in for the night.

"Keep the compass in your pocket at all times, he said, and if you ever get lost in the forest you can use it to find your way home."

"Aye, aye, Captain," Timmy said with a smile as he threw some kindling onto the fire.

A few hours relaxing in front of a cozy fire roasting marshmallows and telling stories made it easy for the family to settle in on their first night in their new home. Their long journey had ended, and everyone in the Paige family was looking forward to sleeping in their new bedrooms. The rooms weren't quite ready, but they were a welcome sight after traveling through the brutal storm.

Before the sun had a chance to rise, a crack of lightning woke the children. They stumbled sleepily over to the rain-beaded window in the far corner of the room and looked down into the yard below. Strange sounds echoing through the air prompted Timmy to press his ear against the window. Faint cries were coming from a pile of branches lying on top of a rusted old bicycle beneath the window. Something was pinned underneath and trying desperately to break free. The children ran quickly down the hall to wake up their mom and dad.

"Dad, Dad. Wake up. Something is moving in the yard," Timmy muttered, shaking his father's arm.

Monica and Michael followed their children back to the bedroom and peered out the window to see if the children were letting their imagination run away with them. To their surprise, there really was something trapped in the yard. Michael ran back to his room to grab the blanket off his bed to shelter him from the heavy rain until he reached the rusted old bike. As he carefully lifted the bike and looked underneath, he saw a frightened little kitten mewing sadly.

Immediately, he scooped up the kitten and brought it inside to warm the soaking wet black and gray striped tabby by the dwindling fire. Timmy grabbed one of the empty boxes and put a blanket inside to keep the kitten safe and warm while his father threw more logs on the fire.

"Honey, why don't you go back to bed? The children and I will take care of the kitten," Michael said.

Monica smiled sleepily at everyone and turned to walk back upstairs.

"What happened to his mommy and daddy?" Jackie asked, gently stroking the kitten.

"They probably were lost in the storm, honey. Now, you better go back to sleep. It's very late."

"But I wanna sleep with our new kitty by the fireplace."

"Okay, but just for tonight. Don't forget tomorrow is Mommy's birthday and I'm going to need your help with her surprise."

The children stayed up as long as they could with their frightened little kitten until they couldn't keep their eyes open any longer. The next morning, the children put a plate of tuna fish inside the box and carried the kitten up to Timmy's room and placed it under his bed.

"Hey, Jackie. There's a bunch of old books in the room down the hall. Let's go see if we can find a name for our new kitty. Come on, it's time for a piggyback ride."

Jackie climbed on her brother's back and started singing her favorite lullaby, "Twinkle, Twinkle, Little Star," all the way down the hall.

Inside the room, Timmy guided his finger over the titles of every book on the shelf, one by one. A Christmas Carol, Gulliver's Travels, Moby Dick, and Oliver Twist, then suddenly, a cracking sound caught his attention.

"Watch out!" he shouted as the top shelf gave way and the books fell to the floor. He pulled his shirt up to cover his mouth and reached out to grab Jackie's hand.

A mushroom cloud of dust came crashing down all over the room. Jackie sneezed and sneezed and sneezed. As soon as it settled, Timmy fanned the books out like a deck of cards and began to wipe away the cobwebs from a book that caught his eye. It was a worn-out copy of Romeo and Juliet, which just happened to be one of his mother's favorite romantic stories.

"Look, Jackie, I just found the perfect gift for Mom 's birthday. I think I saw wrapping paper in one of the boxes in my closet."

They quickly ran back to his room, but there was not one scrap of wrapping paper to be found. Jackie sat down on the floor and began to pout as her eyes filled with tears. Without a moment to spare, Timmy came up with a plan to wrap the book with a torn-out page from his little sister's coloring book.

He explained to her that the love-smitten Romeo in Romeo and Juliet was one of their mother's favorite characters, and that the picture Jackie colored all by herself would make their mother's birthday extra special. Jackie began to spin like a top with excitement until she became so dizzy that she plopped right down on the floor, giggling.

Soon after, their father quietly entered the bedroom and whispered to the children to keep their mother busy for an hour while he decorated the entire downstairs for her surprise.

"Let's put her present underneath the kitty's blanket," whispered Timmy. "I bet Mommy will never think to look under there."

Monica was busy unpacking boxes and putting clothes away when the children brought one of their favorite games to her room.

"Mommy, sit on the bed and close your eyes."

When she sat down, they placed a blindfold over her eyes. Pin the Tail on the Donkey was the perfect way to keep her busy until, after a while, Michael leaned his head in the doorway and signaled for them to come downstairs.

"Hold my hand tight, Mommy."

"Where are you taking me?"

"Shh! It's a secret."

The children guided her all the way down the stairs until they reached the living room. As they removed the blindfold from her eyes, Monica let out a gasp of pure excitement.

"So, this is what you all have been up to" she said.

While his father showered their mother with gifts, Timmy quickly ran back upstairs to get the present hidden underneath the kitty's blanket. Jackie patiently sat at her mother's feet with her eyes fixed toward the top of the stairs until her brother returned with their special gift. When Timmy reappeared, Jackie started bouncing up and down.

"Here, Mommy, this one. Open this one," she said.

Monica carefully unwrapped the beautiful picture colored by her daughter and was amazed to find one of her favorite books inside.

"My goodness! Where did you find this?" she asked.

"It's a secret," Jackie snickered.

Just then, everyone could hear the sounds of scampering paws. It was their unexpected family member, having fun while wrestling the strewn-about wrapping paper.

"Timmy, have you and Jackie come up with a name for this little guy yet?" Monica asked.

"Not yet," they both shouted from across the spacious family room.

It was then that she decided to name him Monty, which was short for Montague from the love story between Romeo Montague and Juliet Capulet. Monty seemed to like his new name and began rubbing his face against Jackie's leg, purring.

"What's that red stuff on Monty's belly?" Jackie wanted to know.

"I don't know, honey. It's probably paint from the old bicycle that was lying on top of him during the storm."

At that moment, Michael carefully walked into the room with a delicious chocolate birthday cake with candles whose flames looked like they were dancing every time he took a step. Jackie hurried to climb on the chair next to her mother as she made her wish and blew out the candles.

Then everyone got to enjoy a sweet slice of chocolate cake with strawberry ice cream, whipped cream, and a juicy red cherry on the top, while Monty continued with his playful romp through the wrapping paper that was scattered about the living room floor.

The family spent the rest of the day playing games and listening to Timmy's endless stories of make believe, while Monty proudly pranced around his newfound family home.

"Now, children, Monica finally said, "it's getting late and time to get ready for bed. Tomorrow is your first day of school."

Deep into the night, the children could hear the sounds of shutters banging and floorboards creaking as if ghosts were roaming the halls. Jackie grabbed her doll and ran huffing and puffing straight into her brother's room at the end of the hall next to the servant's quarters.

"Don't worry, Jackie. You can stay with me."

"Where's Monty?" she cried.

"I bet as soon as you get under the covers, Monty will come in and surprise you. Now, close your eyes and go to sleep."

Soon after, Monty pranced into the room and burrowed himself between Jackie and Timmy.

Early the next morning, Mother Nature did her very best to lend a helping hand by piercing every window throughout the house with her beautiful sunshine. The children could feel the warmth from the sun wrap around them as they scrambled to get ready for school.

Thankfully, the tantalizing smell of her favorite breakfast sausage and blueberry pancakes shaped like Mickey Mouse lingered in the air, bringing comfort to an otherwise scary first day of school.

While the children finished their breakfast, Monica prepared their lunch boxes and slipped in a little love note before the bus arrived.

"I'm going to need your help with your sister before you leave," Monica said quietly to Timmy.

Timmy nodded and held his sister in his arms while his mother set up the car seat for Jackie's first day at pre-kindergarten. Jackie wrapped her arms around her brother's neck and began to whimper every time he tried to place her in the car seat.

"Let go, Jackie. I have to leave," he said as the bus driver honked the horn for the second time.

Monica had to pull her away from Timmy as he rushed to get on the bus. She watched the tears drip down her daughter's face.

"It's ok, honey, she said. "Today's the day you meet all your new friends."

Little by little, Jackie's smile began to grow as they turned into the school parking lot and she saw a crowd of children laughing and singing in line. As soon as her mother unbuckled the seatbelt, Jackie squirmed her way out of the car seat and rushed to get in line.

Soon after, the morning bell rang, signaling the school day was about to begin. Monica patiently waited with the other parents until the last child entered the school.

At that moment, she decided to drive into the small town of Calico and find the street known as Sailors Row to gather some items from the old-fashioned general store that once housed pirates fleeing the hangman's noose. As she walked through the cobblestone streets, she sensed excitement in the air. The antique shops, art galleries and mouthwatering smell of home-baked bread filled the air as she entered the village square.

She had no idea that the news of her arrival would have spread so quickly. Within minutes, the local shopkeepers welcomed their new neighbor with home-baked breads, apple pie, and fresh vegetables, which made her feel right at home. Her entire morning was spent on a tour around the town given by her neighbors and a blessing given by Father Anthony, the community pastor.

Then the sudden sound of the church bell alerted her to gather up all the generous gifts from her new friends and head back to pick up her little girl.

Back at school, Timmy spent his day planning another scavenger hunt in the hopes of finding the name of the pirate who left his compass behind. But the school day seemed to move as slow as a snail until the sound of the three o'clock bell rang through the halls. He sat staring at his compass the entire bus ride home, trying to imagine what adventures it had seen.

The sound of his sister's voice yelling out his name as the bus pulled up to his stop brought him back to reality. She was waiting on the front porch to show her big brother the crayon-colored family picture she made on her first day of school.

"Hey, Jackie. Who's that furry little guy in your picture?"

"It's Monty, silly," Jackie said with a twinkle in her eye.

He was surprised not to see Monty. After all, the front door made a long screeching noise when opened, which would surely attract his attention, but Monty never showed up to play. Where could he be? His sister raced around the house, looking desperately into every nook and cranny but Monty was nowhere to be found. Timmy knew the odds of finding him would be slim, because Monty was still very small and could easily hide anywhere in the house without being seen.

A few minutes later, he found his sister curled up in a ball crying in the corner of one of the rooms and whispered in her ear.

"Don't worry Jackie. He'll come back," said Timmy as he sat down beside her.

"But what if he ran away and we never see him again?" she said as the tears ran down her face.

"How about tomorrow, we camp out in front of the fireplace with a plate of tasty tuna fish for Monty?" he said in a comforting tone.

"OK," she said softly whimpering.

Timmy reached over and took her by the hand back to her room down the hall. He gently kissed her forehead and tucked her into bed for the night.

Chapter 3

THE NEXT MORNING, JACKIE came skipping into the dining room with a great big smile on her face and all dressed up for school. She was so excited about her classmate's birthday party that she forgot all about missing her new kitty. Jackie's comical entrance with her school clothes inside out gave everyone a chuckle to start their day. Timmy finished his practice quiz for the math test scheduled that morning and rushed out to the bus stop.

The bus ride took a different route that morning, making the ride to school seem like it was going to take forever to get there. As he entered his classroom, he noticed everyone looking anxious about their first test of the school year, but he didn't care. All he could think about was getting outside and sharing his stories of adventure with his schoolmates.

The hours slowly passed until finally the test was over, and it was time to head to the schoolyard for lunch. Timmy snuck out of line to grab the shady spot under the cherry tree, but someone else had the same idea. As Timmy was unwrapping his sandwich, a big stocky boy with curly orange hair and freckles came out from behind the tree.

"Well, well, well, look who we have here. That ham sandwich looks awfully good," the boy said in a sinister tone of voice.

Billy McDevitt was the town bully and an angry fellow who took pleasure in the suffering of others. Before Timmy could take his first bite, Billy snatched his lunch right out of his hand and pushed him to the ground. Timmy jumped up and tried to defend himself, but he was outnumbered by Billy's gang who circled Timmy like a group of sharks waiting to eat their prey.

The sound of their laughter grew louder as he watched Billy eat his ham sandwich right in front of him with a smirk on his face that churned Timmy's innards.

The school bell put an abrupt end to the lunchtime that Timmy had planned, leaving him no choice but to return to his class with an empty stomach. While his classmates sat down in their assigned seats, he went straight to his teacher to tell her what happened.

"Some boy in the schoolyard took my sandwich."

"Sit back in your seat, young man. All right children, take out your colored pencils and draw me your favorite animal."

All Timmy could do was just sit there, shaking his head and wondering why his teacher would not listen to him. A few minutes later, his insides began to rumble like an earthquake, prompting the teacher to send him to the school nurse to get some medicine for his upset stomach. He asked the nurse why his teacher wouldn't listen, but she too had nothing to say about it.

By the time he arrived back at his classroom, the children were already packing up their school bags and getting ready to head for home.

Timmy struggled with the thought of how he would survive every day at school with the scary boy who stole his lunch right out from under his nose. He didn't yet know that Billy was the last of a long line of troublemakers who tormented everyone who crossed their path. He had the power to steal your lunch money and make everyone watch as he made you beg him to stop. Every boy and girl feared him, and Billy loved every minute of it.

Timmy's entire bus ride home was spent sitting on the edge of his seat until he was home safely. Jackie was waiting at the dinner table putting a new dress on her doll when he entered the front door. There was southern fried chicken, corn on the cob, sweet potato mashed potatoes, cornbread and so much laughter, he forgot all his troubles.

Soon after, Monty came running out from behind the basement door and made a mad dash to greet Timmy. The purrs and kisses from Monty were the moment that proved he was officially part of the family, and the children couldn't have been happier.

Unfortunately, Timmy's moment of happiness was short lived, because the town bully zeroed in on his every move. Week after week Timmy tried to dodge the evil that lurked around every corner, but nothing seemed to stop "Billy the Bully" from invading his personal space. He was like a mad dog in search of his next victim and Timmy was his target. But to Timmy's surprise, in the midst of all his anguish, a great idea emerged. He decided to try it out the next day at school.

At the crack of dawn, Timmy rushed down to the kitchen before anyone was awake and made an extra sandwich for lunch. He was determined to outsmart the bully at his own game, but he wondered whether his tactical maneuver would win the war against his archenemy.

The day started out like any other with homeroom assignments, a short quiz, and a new book to be read by the end of the week. Timmy spent the entire morning fixated on the second hand of the clock as it ticked away like a time bomb. The excitement of hearing the lunch bell ring had been replaced by his worst fear. He was about to become Billy's latest victim.

Lunchtime finally arrived and he was ready to put his plan into action. He grabbed his jacket off the classroom hook and followed his classmates in single file into the hallway. With a flick of the wrist, the door to the schoolyard was open and the mad rush to eat lunch and play with friends began to unfold.

TIMMY'S WHOLE BODY was shaking as he waited under the cherry tree for his nemesis to arrive. The enemy came through the front gate and approached him with that same sinister smile and glare in his eyes.

"Give me your sandwich now, Timmy boy."

Timmy reached into his school bag and handed his lunch over to Billy, who unrolled the brown paper bag and pulled out the PBJ inside.

"You better have a ham sandwich next time or else!"

"Billy is going to clobber you," laughed one of the boys,

The loyal gang of troublemakers who followed Billy around like lost puppies laughed as they pushed Timmy back and forth until he tripped and landed on the ground. But within seconds, Billy and the boys became interested in a scuffle happening on the other side of the schoolyard. As soon as they were out of sight, Timmy quickly pulled out his ham sandwich and ate his lunch.

Finally, he had outwitted the town bully. He thought his troubles were over once and for all. Some weeks passed without any more problems until one day, another soldier of "Billy the Bully" found out about Timmy's little secret. Timmy trembled with fear at the thought that soon his enemy would learn the truth.

Surprisingly, his anxiety melted away as he walked through the front door at home and saw Monty waiting to play at the top of the stairs. He spent the next few hours playing fetch with Monty and pretending that everything was back to normal. It wasn't until his head hit the pillow that reality set in. Billy was coming after him and there was nothing, he could do to stop it. He tossed and turned all night with worry, trying to figure out a way to escape what Billy had in store for him the next day. But no matter how hard he tried; he couldn't stop the thoughts that were torturing his mind.

It was very early in the morning, but Jackie was already up and sitting on her brother's bed holding her tummy as if it were turning upside down.

"What's the matter Jackie?" asked Timmy worriedly.

"My belly hurts," she cried.

"Are you hungry? Let's go down to the kitchen and I'll make you a peanut butter and jelly sandwich."

A few minutes later, Monica came in and let out a burst of laughter. Jackie looked like a chipmunk with a big clump of jelly on the side of her mouth and her cheeks full of PBJ.

"I guess you already had breakfast, so run upstairs and get ready for school."

As Timmy stood looking out his bedroom window, he could see the glimmer of the old yellow school bus coming over the horizon. He quickly grabbed his schoolbag off the bed and fled down the stairs to grab a banana before he rushed out the door. The lump in his throat grew bigger as the bus pulled over at each stop. He knew he was outnumbered and that it was only a matter of time before he would have to face Billy and his motley crew.

The children gathered their belongings as the bus made its final turn into the school parking lot. As Timmy walked from the back of the bus, he carefully searched all the faces for Billy, but he was nowhere in sight.

The feeling of doom that imprisoned his body lifted as he stepped down off the bus and began sharing his latest adventure stories with his classmates. His excitement made a frightful turn as the sound of screeching brakes from the last bus sent shivers up his spine. Was Billy on that bus? Instantly, his brain switched to high alert, but again, there was still no sign of Billy or his gang of angry thugs. The whole morning was smooth sailing. Timmy finished his homeroom assignments and waited patiently for the lunch bell. And finally, there it was! The bell echoed through the halls, prompting every child to dash for the classroom door. He was excited to see that the hallway was clear of danger and quickly moved to the end of the line.

As the children piled into the schoolyard, he realized he had forgotten his jacket and had to run back to the classroom. He eagerly yanked his jacket off the coat rack in anticipation of sharing another adventure story with his friends. But as he made his way back down the hall, he heard voices coming from around the corner. He had no other choice, but to watch his world end abruptly at the sight of Billy McDevitt.

"Open your jacket," Billy shouted from the other end of the hall.

"No, I won't," Timmy said fearfully as his knees began to buckle under him.

"So, did you think you could fool me Timmy boy?"

Billy's face began to turn a deep bright red as he stalked up the hall like an animal on the hunt for his next meal. His thugs laughed as Billy ripped the sandwich right out of Timmy's inside jacket pocket and took a big bite right in front of him.

"Why can't you just leave me alone?" Timmy said with a noticeable tremble in his voice.

That was the beginning of bruised knees and torn clothing for the big-city boy who was just not strong enough to fight back. Eventually, Timmy ran out of excuses at the dinner table and had to tell his mother and father what was going on at school.

"Timmy, I need you to come into town with me tomorrow," Monica said. "I have a lot of things to pick up and I need a pair of strong hands."

"What are you up to?" Michael asked her quietly.

"Meet me out on the porch and I'll tell you all about it," she replied.

They both grabbed a cup of hot chocolate and sat on the front porch whispering back and forth. Timmy tried to listen through the door, but Jackie kept whining so loud he couldn't hear a thing. She rubbed her eyes and blurted out, "I'm sleepy."

"Shh! I'm trying to hear what Mom and Dad are saying."

But Jackie just kept tugging on his shirt while he tried to listen through the screen door, until he finally gave into her endless sniffling and whimpering.

"Okay. C'mon I'll take you up to bed."

He picked up his baby sister and tucked her into bed then told her one of her favorite bedtime stories until she fell asleep. He nudged her to make sure she was asleep and quietly slid off her bed and turned in for the night.

The next morning, he woke up to the smell of fresh baked blueberry muffins and ran straight to the kitchen where his mother was pouring a hot cup of coffee.

"Are you ready for our big day?"

"I love blueberry muffins."

"I know, honey. I made them just for you."

He grabbed the biggest muffin on top of the pile and took a great big bite. "Gee, Mom. Thanks, a whole bunch."

"I'm going to start the car. Don't forget to grab the list on the table," she said as the kitchen door closed behind her.

It was a beautiful day and everyone in town was out running errands and enjoying the weekend. Their first stop was the produce stand outside the general store and then off to the bakery for some bread right out of the oven. Timmy noticed the samples of artisanal breads on the counter and couldn't resist sharing a thick slice of banana walnut bread with his mom. As he carried the bag of baked goods out of the store, he was met by a few of his schoolmates, who invited him to see a movie later that day. He couldn't wait to see what was playing at the neighborhood cinema.

"We have one more place to stop," Monica said. She gave him a great big smile, placed her hand around her son's shoulder, and walked him across the street to read the sign in the shop window.

"Self-Defense Classes Starting Now. This is awesome!"

"Your dad and I spoke about this last night and we thought you would enjoy taking this class."

Monica didn't waste any time signing her son up for an eighteen-week course in the art of self-defense. Timmy soon learned the discipline he needed to increase his confidence and maintain self-control in times of trouble. It didn't take long before he moved up the ranks to become one of the top students in his class. The small, thin young boy from the big city developed into an opponent ready to take on the Billy McDevitt's of the world.

The last day of his self-defense class was bittersweet, and there was one more question weighing on his mind.

"What do I do if someone tries to hurt me?"

"Well, young man," said the instructor, you have gained great knowledge and skills in this class, but the one thing you must remember in life is that knowledge is power. You must respect the skills you've learned here and only use them to defend yourself against harm."

The instructor congratulated his class of students and sent them on their way, each proudly holding a framed certificate of successful completion of the course.

Once the news of his graduation reached the town bully, it didn't take long for Billy to choose a new victim. As Timmy walked through the schoolyard one day, he came upon a sight all too familiar. Billy and his gang of thugs were taunting another helpless boy.

"Leave him alone. Why don't you pick on someone your own size?" he said as he helped the young boy up off the ground.

The school bell rang just in the nick of time before Billy could inflict any more abuse on the frightened boy. For a split second, Timmy felt he had won the battle against Billy, but he knew all too well that a war with the bully was about to begin. He understood that the day of reckoning was coming, and he would have to stand on his own and face-off with the meanest boy in town.

His late arrival home from school and his lack of appetite struck a chord of worry in his parents.

"What's the matter honey?" his mother inquired.

But Timmy managed to fool them with another story so convincing that they believed it to be true.

"My teacher gave us a surprise test today, and it was really hard. Is it ok if I go to my room and lie down?

"Okay, little man, but next time you and I have to finish our Battleship game."

Timmy's thoughts became so jumbled as the hours passed that not even one idea popped into his head. It was as if someone had taken an eraser and wiped away everything he had learned in the self-defense class. Once again, he tried to escape inside the world of his comic book friends.

As he searched through his collection of storybooks, he stubbed his toe on an old trunk with a broken lock that he assumed the movers had discarded. Inside was the ultimate treasure of mismatched clothing, buckled boots, and old hats left behind by someone whose soul was now a part of the past.

Timmy's imagination began to run wild again as he tried on every piece of clothing in front of his full-length mirror. He would often dress up like Tom Sawyer and pretend he was traveling the Mississippi River with his best friend Huckleberry Finn in search of adventure. He depended on his magical world of make believe to help him forget all his battles with Billy McDevitt, but as hard as he tried that night, he couldn't shake his feeling of gloom.

He reached for his story of Huckleberry Finn and tried desperately to travel back in time. The story of a vagabond who roamed from place to place without a home to call his very own was eerily familiar to Timmy.

After all, he'd learned that Billy was an only child without a mother who drifted as if he were a lost soul trying to fit in any way he could. But his anger at the world around him had grown into physical threats and intimidation for anyone who stood in his way.

Billy would zero in on anyone who was smaller, weaker or easy to intimidate. He was on a mission to ruin your day and his mood would change in an instant. There was no way of knowing where he would strike next or who would be his target. Timmy had only one question on his mind that night. What tricks would Billy have in store for him the next day?

His heart was pounding as the fear of not knowing grew stronger. The words on the page began to blur as he struggled to find a way to confront Billy. His mind was full of confusing thoughts causing his frustration to grow out of control. Ideas would begin to form and then shatter into bits and pieces. He couldn't seem to grasp what was happening all around him and tossed his book across the room. He laid quietly on his bed, staring up at the ceiling until he couldn't bare another thought to enter his mind. The emptiness consumed him until the weight of his eyelids forced his eyes closed.

Timmy drifted into a deep sleep and for awhile he was finally getting some relief. As the hours passed, his dreams began to take him back along the Mississippi River traveling with his friend Huckleberry Finn. The vivid adventure of sitting around a campfire under the light of the moon with his best friend brought comfort to him. Suddenly, the flames of the campfire began to flicker as if someone else was lurking nearby.

A rush of adrenalin began to surge through his body as Billy McDevitt walked out of the shadows in his dream. He called out to his friend Huck, but he was gone and leaving him to face Billy all alone.

"I'm here to teach you a lesson you will never forget Timmy Boy," Billy said as he kicked the sand into the fire.

Timmy ran along the riverbank as fast as he could with Billy trailing right behind him at every turn. Despite his efforts to get away, Billy caught up with him and stopped him in his tracks.

"There's nowhere to go Timmy Boy, and no one can help you now," Billy said as he reached for Timmy's arm.

Timmy awoke shivering from his dream drenched in sweat. He was in disbelief that there was no escape from the hold Billy had over him.

Chapter 4

AS THE GLOW OF THE full moon lassoed the darkened sky, strange sounds came from behind his closet door. Suddenly, a dark and mysterious swirling cloud covered Timmy's body as he climbed off his bed in a trance. He was drawn to his closet like a magnet to metal and was slowly turning the doorknob when the door swung open and knocked him to the floor.

"It is I," said the gigantic shadowy figure standing upright with his paws on his hips, "Monty the Magnificat at your service."

Timmy wiped the tears from his eyes as if to make the image clear and saw the larger-than-life figure of a black- and- gray striped tabby cat wearing bright red glowing mittens smiling down at him.

"What seems to be the trouble, Timmy?" the furry feline said in a deep and frightful voice.

"There's a real scary boy at school who won't stop pushing me around. But how can you talk? I must be dreaming."

He closed his eyes as tight as he could, hoping that the great big tabby cat would disappear. The seconds seemed like hours, but when he slowly opened one eye to sneak a peek, Monty was still there smiling down at him with his piercing green eyes. Timmy was so scared he jumped up onto his bed and threw the covers over his head.

"Well, Timmy, let me tell you a story. I was scared just like you when I was a kitten. One day, when my mom and dad were searching for food for me and my little brother, a scrawny, dirty, smelly, big-mouth street fighter named Butch scared my brother so bad that he ran away, never to be seen again."

A tear came rolling down Monty's long sleek whiskers and landed right on Timmy's nose. Timmy's whole body was frozen as he watched Monty walk back and forth sharing the horrifying events from his past.

"What did you do?"

"Well, for a long time I had to put up with Butch stealing every morsel of food my parents brought back for us. He was a very sneaky cat who would watch and wait until my mom and dad brought back the food and then snatch it up when everyone was asleep. One cold and dreary night, my father woke up early and found Butch scooping up all our food. He confronted Butch and tried to defend our home, but his body was too weak to fight back."

"Boy, oh boy! That's just what Billy does to me every day at school. So, tell me, tell me what happened next."

"My father did everything he could to protect us, but the daily battles with Butch became too much for his weakened body. But he never stopped trying until one night, the angels came and took him away forever."

"Do you mean your father went to heaven?"

"He was taken to a special place known as Rainbow Bridge, where all furry animals who leave this earth wait to be reunited with all of their loved ones."

"What happened to Butch?"

"Well, for the longest time, he seemed to have vanished into thin air, until one rainy night in May we noticed a dark and dirty figure slowly creeping toward our new home. There was that same sickening street smell of a desperate tomcat hunting his next prey.

My fear became more real when the cat drew near. It was the notorious Butch who had come back to terrorize anyone in his path. I froze, like I did when I was a kitten, and watched in horror as he shoved my mother into a muddy puddle of water.

Suddenly, he heard a scuffle of what might be a new threat in town and went to check out his competition. Without a moment to spare, my mother grabbed my paw and we escaped in search of a safe place to live."

"What happened next?"

"One day while I was hunting for food, Butch found our new hiding place. He fiercely swept everything in his path over the broken bridge. Sadly, my mother was lying weak and hungry beneath the garbage on the city streets and was unable to defend herself. When I returned, she was gone, and I never saw her again. Soon after, Butch came back for more."

"What did you do?"

"I faced him head on."

"Were you scared?"

"Yes, I was, but I didn't let him know it. We scuffled and clawed our way to the top of the bridge when suddenly my mittens began to glow and light up the sky. I felt a powerful force inside me, and for the first time, I was not afraid. As we stood balancing on the edge of the truss bridge, a howling gust of wind swept us backward against the beams. We fixed our eyes on the clouds above as they swirled all around us and the thunderous voice of my father echoed across the sky. He said, 'My son, do not become like the evil tomcat who stands before you."

"Wow! You have magic mittens?"

"As I looked deep into Butch's eyes, I could see the anger that controlled his every move melt away and leave behind a frightened tomcat who was all alone without a friend in the world. I ended the fight and watched Butch run off into the darkness never to be seen again. Now, you better get to sleep, you have school in the morning."

"But where are you going?"

"There is still a lot of work to be done, my friend."

"Will I ever see you again Monty?"

"Don't worry, I will always be watching over you."

Chapter 5

THE NEXT MORNING, TIMMY woke up staring anxiously at his bedroom closet, trying to get up the nerve to look inside. Without making a sound, he tip toed over to the closet door and slowly wrapped his hand around the bronze-plated doorknob. As he carefully turned the knob, a sudden movement from behind the closet door startled him. He yanked open the door out of sheer fright and found Monty snuggled on top of an old pair of red mittens on the closet shelf. "Gosh! What a crazy dream," Timmy said to himself as he tried to catch his breath.

Before he could make sense of what had happened in the middle of the night, Monty leaped from the closet and sailed straight into his basket of dirty clothes.

"You are one crazy cat," Timmy said with a silly laugh as he headed down the stairs.

Monty scampered right behind him toward the breakfast table, hoping to snag a treat from his new family.

"Are you all right?" Monica asked Timmy as he pulled out his chair.

"Monty the Magnificat came to see me, and he was so big that the tips of his ears touched the ceiling! He told me a story about an evil tomcat named Butch who came to town to steal everything he could from anyone who got in his way, but Monty had magic mittens that gave him power to stop Butch," Timmy abruptly ran out of steam.

"That is a very unusual dream, but you better eat your breakfast before the bus arrives."

Timmy wasn't at all surprised that no one believed his story, because he too wondered if Monty the Magnificat truly existed or whether he was just a figment of his own vivid imagination.

After breakfast, he ran back up to his room to get the red mittens from his closet. The bus was running late, so he tucked them into his inner jacket pocket and played with Monty until he had to leave for school.

"Hurry! The bus is here. You're going to be late."

"Ok, Mom. I'm coming."

While on the bus, he could not stop thinking about Monty, and he wanted desperately to put the magic mittens to the test. He looked all around to make sure he wasn't being watched and took the red mittens out of his jacket pocket. A powerful surge of energy ran through his body, making him feel as brave as Monty did when he confronted Butch on top of the bridge.

But the feeling disappeared as soon as the bus pulled into the school parking lot. He took the mittens off and hid them back in his jacket pocket so his friends would be none the wiser.

His teacher was checking attendance and handing out their first task of the day when he entered the room. The entire morning would be spent writing about someone special in your life. This time, Timmy had a whopper of a story to tell. As he wrote down the detailed account of his encounter with the giant cat with magic mittens, it became clear that his visit from Monty was not a dream but as real as the nose on his face. But as he searched the room for someone he could trust, he realized that everyone would think it was just another one of his wild stories.

He decided it was best to never tell a soul about Monty and his secret powers. He quickly pulled out another piece of paper and wrote a short story about his journey from the big city and the storm that nearly drove his family off the road. His thoughts were in a race against the clock as the teacher made her way around the room collecting all the stories. He had only seconds left to jot down the last word on the page before his teacher reached his desk.

"Pencils down, everybody, and straighten up your desks," the teacher said in a rush to break for lunch.

As Timmy put his pencil down and looked up from his desk, he locked eyes with the most beautiful girl in his class. Her never-ending smile took his breath away every time she looked his way. So far, it was the perfect day, and for once he prayed that his school day would never end.

He stood on an old milk crate under the cherry tree, waiting for his schoolmates to gather around to listen to his tales of adventure and voyages beyond their wildest dreams. After all, he was a storyteller with an exceptional flair for detail who captivated everyone around him with his tales, especially in a town known to have been inhabited centuries before by swashbuckling pirates who swaggered in from time to time on a mission to wreak havoc after a long sea journey.

"Tell us more," one of his classmates shouted.

"Meet me here tomorrow and I will tell you what happened next."

The rest of the afternoon, Timmy sat daydreaming about Monty the Magnificat and his triumph against the most feared tomcat known to Cat's Eye Alley. His preoccupation with his magical friend continued until the thump of a heavy book hitting the classroom floor snapped him back into reality. He quickly straightened up his desk and ran to the front of the class to be first in line for the bus.

Everyone was whispering and wondering why Billy McDevitt had not been in school that day. After all, Billy would never pass up the chance to pick on Joey Matheson. During the bus ride home, Timmy noticed the streets were unusually quiet, which made him wonder what evil deeds were taking place and who was going to be Billy's next victim. But all his worries were put to an end as soon as the bus made its final stop.

The sight of Monty straddled on top of the front screen door with his nails clearly dug into the frame tickled Timmy's funny bone and even had the bus driver laughing as he pulled away. Timmy rushed up to his bedroom to start on his homework before dinner but noticed his compass was missing from its brown leather pouch.

While he was busy pulling his clothes out of every drawer in search of the compass, Monty entered the room, mewing for attention and ready to play. But the sudden popping of a car backfiring sent him racing around the room in a frenzy until he ran out of gas. Timmy heard the clanging of the dinner plates as his mother set the table and decided to put his search on hold.

"Where's Monty?" Jackie asked as Timmy slid down the banister of the staircase.

"Oh, he heard a loud noise outside and is hiding under my bed."

"Can I go play with him after dinner, Mommy?"

"How about we all watch The Wizard of Oz after dinner?"

"Can I sit next to you, Mommy?"

"How about you sit in the middle of me and Daddy?"

"Yippeeeeee!" Jackie yelled.

After dinner, Timmy asked, "Is it ok if I go to my room?"

"Sure honey, go right ahead, but don't stay up too late."

"But it's the weekend."

"I know, but you haven't been sleeping well and you need to get your rest."

One of Timmy's books had fallen off the shelf onto the floor. Although he had not yet read the story of Peter Pan, he felt a new adventure could be just what he needed. He was instantly captivated by the story of a mischievous young boy who could fly and who never grows up. He was excited to find that Peter Pan lived on the small island of Neverland, where he spent his childhood having adventures as the leader of a gang of "Lost Boys."

Throughout the story, similarities between the character of Peter Pan and Billy McDevitt began to emerge. With every turn of the page, Timmy could envision Billy leading his gang of thugs through the streets of Sailors Row on a mission to recruit more followers. The powerful images Timmy created in his mind stirred his curiosity long enough to finish the story before he fell asleep.

The next morning, he awoke to the sound of chimes and bells coming from below his window. He ran to see what it was and stubbed his toe on the compass that must have fallen on the bedroom floor.

"Ouch!" Timmy said in a frustrated tone.

But when he saw his father standing underneath his bedroom window next to a brand-new bike, he forgot all about his toe and rushed down to the backyard.

"Boy, oh boy, can I ride my new bike into town to show my friends?"

"That's a great idea, but just make sure your home in time for dinner."

The sun was out, and the weather was perfect for a ride through the coastal town. Timmy was bubbling over with excitement to show off his new bike as he headed straight to the park. The sound of his schoolmates playing dodge ball was like music to his ears as he approached the south entrance. The game came to a screeching halt as he popped a wheelie right in front of the boys.

"Hey Timmy, is that a new bike?" one of the boys shouted.

"Yeah. My dad surprised me first thing this morning."

"Let's all get our bikes and meet at Mr. Lemon's," another one of the boys suggested.

Timmy reached into his back pocket and pulled out his trusty compass. The magnetized needle maintained a course of due south as he headed toward the most popular hang out in town. The cool, sweet taste of homemade ice cream sundaes with whipped cream and rainbow sprinkles was on the menu. The boys all chipped in their spare change and treated their new friend to an ice cream cone. As he took the last bite of his vanilla and chocolate swirl, a brilliant idea came popping out of his mouth.

"Hey, I have an idea. Let's go on a scavenger hunt."

"What's that?" said one of the boys as he slurped down the last of his milkshake.

"Well, you pick a special place and make a list of things to hide there. On the day of the hunt, you divide your friends into teams and give them each a list of the things to find. Whoever finds everything on the list in time will win a prize at the end of the hunt. The prize can be whatever you want it to be, like movie tickets, money for ice cream, or a new video game, stuff like that."

"That sounds really cool. Do you want to see our secret hideaway?" one of the boys mentioned on the way out of the ice cream parlor.

"Wow! Let's go," Timmy said with a grin.

The boys rode their bikes down a dirt road behind the ice cream parlor until they reached a cluster of trees marked with an X about three miles away from town. In a large clearing beyond the trees was their very own fort, built out of old tree limbs and worn out sails from the shipyard. One of the boys pulled a heavy backpack off the back of his bike and finished placing the last section of rocks around the fire pit where they planned to roast hot dogs and marshmallows. Timmy stood in the center of the clearing with his trusty compass and marked his location for a safe return home.

The boys gathered around and listened to their new friend tell a story that would not only seal their friendship, but also bring fantasy to life for these adventurous young boys. He described how the infamous pirate Blackbeard captured a French slave ship back in 1717, later known as Queen Anne's Revenge, and refitted it with forty guns. The enormous firepower led to a blockade at the port of Charleston, South Carolina, where no one could enter or leave until his demands for a large chest of medicine were met.

"I'll be the captain of this pirate lair and you are all my mates. What say you?" Timmy shouted to his trusted band of brothers.

"Aye, aye, Captain," the boys roared as they raised their fists into the air.

He led the boys into his world of make believe where they all became pirates on a quest for hidden treasure.

While gathering kindling for the fire, the boys discovered a brand-new trail that led them to a mountainside. A gaping hole on the side of the mountain let in enough sunlight to light the entrance as the boys followed their fearless captain deep inside the cave.

Once inside, they stumbled upon an old campsite where they spent a long time sitting around and listening to their adventurous friend spin tales about legendary pirates who once sailed the seven seas. The boys were having so much fun that they didn't notice the sun was going down until the light inside the cave began to dim.

"We better hurry back before it gets dark," said one of the boys.

It was beginning to get cold as they rushed in single file toward the entrance to the cave, but when they got there, they discovered it was a dead end. Somehow, they had taken a wrong turn and ended up inside another tunnel.

"Oh no! Does anybody remember which tunnel we took?" one of the boys shouted.

Timmy pulled out his compass. "All we have to do is follow my compass to the tunnel that points north, and we should be able to find our way back," he said.

The boys clustered around him as he pointed his compass toward each cave. For a split second, the needle seemed to be stuck and then it began to twitch rapidly first to the east, and then back and forth until it reached closest to the north and stopped.

"Ok. This is the one. Let's hurry!"

THEY RAN AS FAST AS they could out of the cave and back to their secret fort. One of the boys told Timmy that he could save time by taking a shortcut through the park. He gladly took his advice, but as he approached the last mile, he saw a crowd of kids playing under a large oak tree. The closer he got the more uneasy he felt, because the faces were those of Billy's friends.

In the distance, he could see Billy lock eyes with him, but it was too late to turn back. All the boys came rushing toward him from every direction, leaving him with no choice but to stand his ground. They surrounded his bike and began having a tug of war over who would take his new bike home.

"Give me your bike or else," one of the boys shouted.

"No, I won't. I'm not afraid of any of you."

They pulled and pushed Timmy until Billy snuck behind and surprised him. Timmy held on to his handlebars as tight as he could until all the boys yanked him to the ground and held him down against his will.

As he lay there struggling to get free, Billy jumped on the bike and rode off into the sunset. The gang of thugs raced after him, leaving Timmy all alone in the middle of the park trying desperately to come up with a story, because he was too ashamed to admit what really happened to his new bike. He ran as fast as he could to get home before his dad arrived.

It didn't take long before Jackie fell asleep snuggled in the safety of her brother's arms. Once again, Timmy found himself wide awake and staring up at the ceiling, trying to figure out what to do about Billy. He tossed and turned all night long until he found the courage to tell his father the truth and admit that he was still too weak to go head to head with Billy McDevitt.

The smell of coffee and bacon and eggs was in the air as he walked his sister down the hall the next morning. He felt like there was a hundred pounds wrapped around his legs as he approached the breakfast table.

"Dad, I have something to tell you."

"What is it, son?"

He began to shake. "My bike was stolen by this big bully in the park last night."

"Are you talking about Billy McDevitt again?"

"I'm sorry, Dad. I tried to get away, but there were too many of them."

"Don't worry, Timmy, it isn't your fault."

His father went straight to the McDevitt house to get the bicycle, while Timmy stayed home wrestling with his stomach that was tied up in knots.

A pungent smell of paint from the garage area grew stronger as Michael reached the side of the McDevitt house. Billy was putting the finishing touches on a bicycle that looked identical to the one he bought his son.

"What a nice bike you have there, Billy."

"Oh! Hi, Mr. Paige." Billy just pulled another one of his lies out of his pocket and explained he was painting over the scratches from his old bike. "How do you like the color?"

"Billy, I need to speak with your father."

"Oh! He's not home right now."

Michael knew all too well that the bike belonged to his son, but there was nothing he could do except turn around and head for home.

Timmy paced back and forth in front of his bedroom window until he could see his father coming over the hill. His whole body filled with his failure to conquer his demons when he realized his father was empty handed. Timmy stayed in his room, reading story after story, hoping to escape from the turmoil that followed him day and night without fail. Suddenly, he could hear his father's footsteps coming toward his room and he quickly pulled the blanket over his head.

"It's all right, son. Don't worry. Things have a way of working themselves out. How about a game of Battleship?"

"Great Idea," Timmy replied.

"Get ready. I'm going to win this time."

"Oh no you're not," Timmy protested as he rushed past his father down the stairs into the living room.

The battle of wills between father and son was a great distraction for Timmy. Michael was a fierce competitor challenging his son at every turn. But against all odds, Timmy sank the final battleship and won the game.

Chapter 6

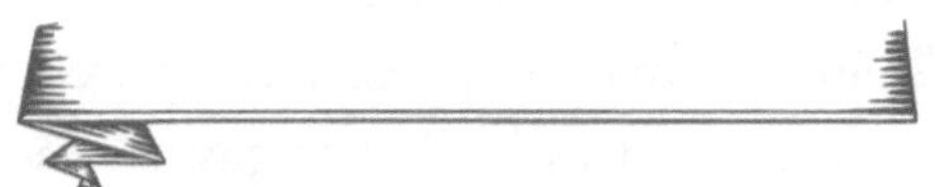

ONCE AGAIN, A DREAMLIKE state imprisoned Timmy's body as the clock struck the midnight hour. At the foot of his bed stood none other than Monty the Magnificat, the larger-than-life mysterious feline. The echo of Monty's deep vibrating voice shook Timmy's bed as he listened to Monty's plea.

"Timmy, I need your help down at the old shipyard."

"Why do you want to go there?"

"I heard my mother might be held captive there."

"But I thought you said that Butch threw her off the bridge."

"Well, my friend, if you were given a second chance to find someone you thought was lost forever, wouldn't you at least want to find out the truth?"

"I guess so. Can I wear your magic mittens?"

"My friend, you are already wearing them."

Suddenly, Timmy felt an unusual sensation travel through his body, and he stared in amazement as his hands gave off a bright, ruby-red glow. He felt like one of the superheroes in his comic book stories. He grabbed his trusty compass out of his schoolbag and climbed up the back of Monty's hind leg until he reached the black leather silver-studded collar wrapped around his neck.

"Hold on tight," Monty said as he swiftly soared through the sky.

"Wow! This is the coolest thing ever," Timmy said, gazing at the town below.

"Shhh! We're almost there."

The moon lit up the sky as they traveled over the great forest of hidden secrets. Feline cries could be heard throughout their journey, as Monty shared his stories about the most evil tomcat that ever roamed the earth.

"Simon is the most sinister and most feared soldier of evil who will kidnap you and force you to live a life of hard labor chained below the deck of his ship."

"Don't worry, Monty. The power of the magic mittens will protect us from Simon."

Suddenly, they could hear the painful cries of the slaves getting louder as they approached the stranded ship that had run aground three miles offshore.

"We have to move quickly before we are spotted by Simon's evil crew."

Timmy braced himself as Monty glided along the water until he reached the front of the ship.

"Look, Timmy! There he is, sitting on the kings' throne. Whatever you do, don't let him see you or it could mean the end for both of us."

They hid in the shadows alongside the bow of the ship until Simon had filled his belly with the catch of the day. It felt like an eternity as they watched and waited to make their move.

"The time has come, my friend," Monty finally whispered.

"Hold on tight and don't make a sound," he added.

Timmy straddled Monty's back as he climbed up the bow of the ship and hid behind a pile of fish barrels left behind by Simon's crew.

"I have an idea. You stay here while I search for my mother below deck and stomp your foot three times if someone is coming."

"Ok. But you better hurry in case Simon wakes up."

A familiar scent touched the tip of Monty's nose as he opened the grated hatchway between decks. It was all the proof he needed that his mother was alive and somewhere among the tortured souls below. He carefully searched every corner below the ship until he set his eyes on a frightened and ragged-looking cat caged underneath a pile of empty broken barrels.

"I have been waiting so long for you to find me," the cat whispered with a trembling voice.

"I thought you were gone forever, Mother."

"Don't cry, dear. I always knew you would find me someday."

Monty quickly pulled on the rusted chain and released the shackles from all who had fallen victim to Simon and his band of thieves. But just as they were making their escape, a bolt of lightning struck the bow of the ship, awakening Simon and knocking Timmy over the barrels of gutted fish. Out of the shadows came Simon's private army of feline street fighters, who forced him to kneel at the foot of their king's powerful throne.

Meanwhile, Monty escaped with his mother into the forest for safety, while the other stray cats ran for their lives. Timmy found himself alone and at the mercy of Simon and his motley crew.

"You are sentenced to be my personal slave and do my bidding as I see fit. Now, get him out of my sight," Simon ordered as he cracked his whip across the deck.

Timmy struggled to get away as he was dragged below deck, but it was no use. He sat in total darkness for a very long time until the light from the full moon came sneaking through a rusted porthole in the side of the vessel. As he strained to look through the fractured glass of the porthole, he could see the shadow of someone climbing aboard the ship. His best friend and comrade had come back to take Simon by surprise.

"Let Timmy go! This fight is between you and me alone," Monty shouted.

Simon let out a nasty laugh and ordered his crew to surround Monty.

"There is no one here to help you now. Take him to join his friend below," Simon ordered.

Simon watched as his loyal crew shoved Monty back and forth until he landed in a pile of barrels containing fish guts.

The heavy barrels gave way, sending Monty and the gutted fish crashing through to the deck below. Out of the darkness came one fearless stray cat who had returned to help Monty save his friend from a life of hard labor. He pulled Monty out of the broken barrel of fish guts and grabbed the keys to unlock the chains that bound Timmy to the floor. Simon became enraged and began yelling orders to capture Monty and his rebellious comrade.

"Get the traitors who dare to come aboard my ship, or you will suffer the same fate," he snarled at his deckhands.

Inside the cargo hold, Monty, Timmy, and the stray could hear scratching and scrabbling noises coming from the side of the ship. They carefully took refuge behind the ladder leading from the steel grate above and waited to fight their way off the ship.

All at once, the grate opened and there stood all the freed slaves. Monty led the charge. Simon sat upon his throne at the bow of the ship, dictating battle orders, when the shouting, screaming, pushing, and shoving came to a sudden halt. A vibrant red glow came shooting from the ship as Monty raised his powerful paws toward the sky and shouted out his final command to Simon.

"Your days of glory are over!"

In an instant, Simon grabbed the rigging line dangling from the mast and swung across the ship to the other side, but not before Monty noticed the jagged scar above his left eye. He recognized the one true enemy from his past, the most dangerous tomcat to ever walk along Cat's Eye Alley. Butch had wanted to be king and almost got away with it, but Monty had been able to chase him out of town. But now Monty must face the infamous thief again, and this time it all must come to an end.

"You can't fool me. I know it's you in disguise Butch, Monty shouted angrily, and it looks like you've been up to your old tricks again."

"So, we meet again my fearless friend," Butch said with a sneer.

Without warning, Butch shot out from the shadows and attacked Monty from behind while his crew shackled his paw to the steel grate. Butch pulled out his trusty whip and marked Monty's back with painfully heavy blows as he struggled to get free. During the tussle, Timmy climbed up the pile of barrels behind Butch and grabbed hold of the whip in mid-air, forcing Butch to his knees. The crew of feline freedom fighters jumped in and overpowered Butch until Monty could be set free.

While Monty and his new comrades were deciding Butch's fate, Butch made his final attempt and lunged at Monty, but he caught his own back paw in a rope tied to the dock. The weight of his body pulled the rope free and he fell backward into the deep, murky water below.

"Please! Help me! I can't swim," Butch screamed as he desperately tried to stay afloat.

He knew that his life was in the hands of the slaves he had once imprisoned and that this could be the end of him forever. Every cat on the ship began to scream cries of victory as the powerful waves dragged Butch under. But without hesitation, Monty threw a life preserver to his enemy to keep him from drowning, which sent the crew into a frenzy of anger.

"Give me your paw," Monty said, leaning over the side of the ship to help Butch aboard.

"You could have let me drown. Why did you save me?" Butch panted.

Monty's mother pranced through the crowd and stood proudly among her fellow ex-slaves as her son handed down his final judgment.

"My mother always believed in giving a second chance to those who lose their way. But you are banished from this ship and you are never to return."

Butch turned around with a tear in his eye and climbed into the dinghy that would take him out to sea.

TIMMY COULD FEEL HIS mother's gentle hand upon his shoulder as she whispered in his ear, "It's time to get ready for school, young man."

"Monty, where are you?" he said, wiping the sleep from his eyes.

"Did you have another dream, honey?"

All he could think about was how Monty saved his own mother from the evilest predator known to Cat's Eye Alley. He told his mother all about it.

"Oh, Timmy, I think it's time I put those comic books away. I think they're playing tricks on you."

"But Mom, Monty the Magnificat is real. He has magic mittens that can light up the sky. Don't you believe me?"

He jumped off his bed and ran over to the closet hoping to find Monty inside, but he wasn't there.

"He was hiding under your bed," Monica said as she cuddled the kitten in her arms.

Timmy leaned over and planted a big kiss on Monty's nose and then gently whispered, "Now stay out of trouble today Monty."

Soon after, he changed into his school clothes and joined his father at the breakfast table.

"Go see if the paper was delivered yet," would you, Timmy?"

The newspaper boy was delivering the paper just as Timmy opened the door. He was startled by the front- page picture of a pirate ship dangling from a huge crane in front of the shipyard.

"Hey, Dad, why is the pirate ship in the paper?"

"I heard a rumor that shipyard authorities are going to develop the area, which means all the ships will be broken down for scrap."

"No! We can't let them do that. Where will Monty's mother and all her friends live?"

"What are you talking about?"

"Last night, I helped Monty save his mother from Butch the evil tomcat. Ohhhh! Never mind, you won't believe me anyway."

"Hurry up and finish your breakfast. The bus will be here any minute."

Timmy gobbled down his last bite of scrambled eggs and headed toward the bus stop.

"Your son had another silly dream last night," Monica said as she poured her husband another cup of coffee.

"Now that explains why he was so upset about the newspaper article."

Monica sighed. "It's a shame they're going to close down the shipyard."

Along the bus route to school, the children noticed an enormous crowd standing outside the Calico courthouse. Apparently, the entire town was in an uproar over the possible closing of the shipyard. After all, an important part of the town's history was about to be erased, along with the past that once defined their community.

The bus slowly made its way through the crowd to the school, and as it reached the entrance, the children let out a gasp of surprise as they read the huge banner with black bold letters saying "SAVE OUR SHIPYARD" that was hanging from the two pillars outside the school. They knew this day was going to be different and they couldn't wait to hear the news.

Without a word, the teacher grabbed the last broken piece of chalk and scribbled the first assignment on the board as the children sat down in their seats. The topic was "How to save the shipyard," and the student with the best idea would get a prize at the end of the day. The excitement in the room was contagious as they raced against the clock to get all their ideas down on paper before the sound of the lunch bell.

Soon after, the children gathered around the cherry tree to hear how Timmy was going to save the shipyard. As he stood on top of a pile of empty milk crates, looking out over the crowd, he blurted out a whopper of an idea that took everyone by surprise.

"Who wants to go on an adventure with me tonight?" he shouted as he jumped down off the milk crates.

The children came from every direction to listen to the secret mission carefully planned by the new kid in town.

"Our parents' votes will not be enough to save the shipyard, but if we add our vote to the total count, we might just have a chance."

"We're just a bunch of kids. I thought our vote doesn't count," a voice shouted from the back of the crowd.

"I thought so too, but that's not true. My dad told me that if we can get everyone to vote it could change everything. Meet me at the town hall as soon as it gets dark. Are you with me?"

The children huddled together and screamed with excitement, "Save the Shipyard! Save the Shipyard!"

The secret mission to save the shipyard was underway with every child on high alert and ready to cast their vote. But the approach of a severe rainstorm drastically hindered travel to the town hall and made some parents unwilling to make the trip. The heavy rains interrupted telephone service, too, leaving Michael to rely solely on the towns people's ability to get their votes in before the gavel hit the sounding block.

"We have to be at the town hall at seven o'clock sharp, right, Dad?"

"Well, then, hurry and finish your dinner, sweetheart, and don't forget your raincoat," his mother replied.

The main road leading in and out of town was almost impassable due to partial flooding and downed power lines. Mother Nature was on the warpath. A full turn out for the final vote scheduled for that evening was unlikely to happen.

"I'm scared, Dad. What if we can't get enough votes?" Timmy said as they drove farther into town.

"We'll give it our best shot, son. We have to at least try," Michael replied as he pulled up to the town hall.

A sinking feeling of despair began to grow in the pit of Timmy's stomach as Michael drove into the empty parking lot. It looked like a scene out of a ghost town, the storm washing away any hope they had of getting enough votes to salvage the shipyard. But they were not about to give up now or let anything stand in their way. Timmy squeezed his father's hand tightly and took a deep breath as they rushed through the rain toward the main entrance doors.

Timmy stood quietly outside the meeting room listening and learning as his father struggled to stop commercial developers from erasing the only historical link associated with the charming seaside town. Michael handed out pictures of influential sea captains and the ships they sailed in the hopes of reminding the town council that Black Sails Bay and its shipyard had repaired and built many of the sea vessels that sailed along the Carolina Intracoastal Waterways.

He explained that the shipyard was a major contributor to the wealth and prosperity of the town back in the 1600s and could be again by reinventing itself as a tourist attraction of historical significance. While the board members were fighting over whether to tear down the shipyard, Timmy quietly entered the room. He stood before the counsel and reached into his raincoat to pull a crumpled piece of paper out of his pocket. With a lump in his throat, he began to read it out loud in the hopes someone was listening.

"Me and my friends will help clean, paint, and fix up the old shipyard after school every day. I promise that we will do a good job and even work extra hard during our summer vacation."

"It's ok, son," said Michael, laying a hand on Timmy's shoulder. "We've done everything we could, but unless the rest of the town shows their support, we just don't stand a chance."

Suddenly, a rush of wind blew the courthouse doors open and behind them were all the local townspeople with their children in hand. Timmy looked up at his father with a great big smile and began to pray under his breath. Silence filled the room until a young child's voice from the back of the crowd shouted out,

"Save the Shipyard!"

"Save the Shipyard!"

The town council members looked at each other in amazement as the room filled beyond its capacity. They realized there was only one decision to be made that night. It became abundantly clear that someone had to head the preservation project and, to his great surprise, the patriarch of the new family in town was selected by a unanimous vote.

The next morning, Michael dropped his son off at school and headed down to the shipyard to assess the damage and begin his first day as preservation engineer. Timmy was amazed to see the line to sign up for the clean-up crew halfway around the school. As he took his spot in line, he noticed something was out of place, but he couldn't put his finger on what was missing until a voice from the crowd fearfully shouted, "Where's Billy? I haven't seen him all morning."

The town bully and his friends were nowhere in sight and everyone knew then that there was trouble brewing. It didn't take long for Timmy to realize that an evil plan was being hatched to slowdown the project, and that he was the only one who could stop Billy before it was too late.

After school, Timmy rushed to meet his father down at the shipyard to warn him, but Michael was held up in a meeting and Timmy was left to handle Billy on his own. Suddenly, from the corner of his eye, he could see his posse of bad boys destroying one of the ships and its contents. He decided right then and there that it was time to challenge Billy. He rushed to climb aboard the ship.

"I can see all your friends doing your dirty work. Where are you, Billy McDevitt?"

"Come out and face me once and for all," Timmy said ready for battle.

Billy appeared from the shadows and was all too eager to make a fool out of Timmy, especially in front of his loyal gang of thugs. He began swinging furiously at Timmy, trying to knock him off his feet, but Timmy's fancy footwork foiled Billy's plan. His self-defense training came to the rescue, because with one jab he was able to knock the bully over the old barrels.

The gang realized Timmy had turned the tables on their fearless leader and began laughing at Billy as he struggled beneath all the barrels.

"Shh! Be quiet and listen," said one of the boys.

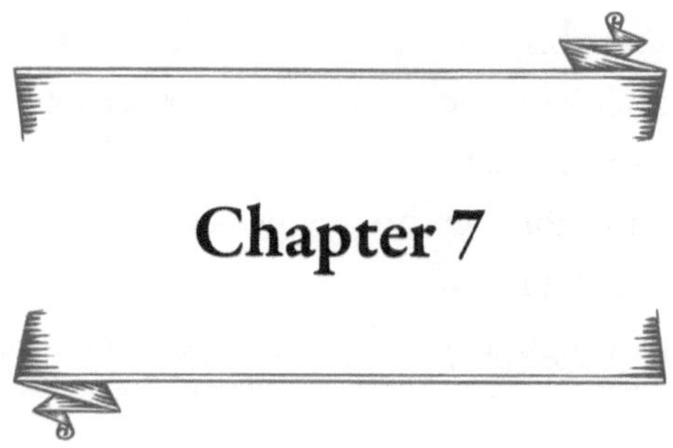

Chapter 7

A STRONG SMELL OF INCENSE flowed through the air as the boys raced to the other side of the ship. Everyone could hear the sound of drums far off in the distance getting louder and louder. The boys wouldn't want to let anyone know, but they were frightened by the stories of voodoo rituals that took place in the forbidden region of Yoruba on the outskirts of town. One of the boys was so scared he yelled out loud, "My big brother told me that a little boy was turned into stone from a voodoo spell and was never seen again." All the boys began to jump ship, leaving Billy McDevitt to fend for himself. Soon he was standing all alone without any backup. He began nervously blubbering in front of Timmy.

"You're not as tough as you have everyone believe, are you?" said Timmy

"Promise you won't tell anyone. Look! There's someone all dressed in white standing on the shoreline," Billy said.

Timmy straddled the rail and climbed down off the ship to get a closer look while Billy dangled from a ladder made of old remnants of rope.

"I don't think this is such a good idea," Billy whispered as he made his way down the ladder.

"This is so cool. I read about Yoruba in a book I found back at my house," Timmy whispered.

"Don't let her see you or she'll turn you into stone," Billy cried.

"Just be quiet and stay close behind me."

Suddenly, Timmy tripped over a pile of wood held together with mooring lines and the chanting abruptly stopped. Before they could get away, they found themselves looking into the piercing red eyes of the high priestess of Yoruba.

"Come here. Do not be afraid," said Agbenyaga.

"What are we going to do now?" Billy whimpered as he grabbed Timmy by the arm.

The woman took both boys and sat them down next to her at a circle of fire. One by one the people around the fire passed a handmade smoking pipe until it reached Timmy. The priestess said, "If you smoke this magic herb, you will be protected from any danger that awaits you."

Both boys were unable to resist the force of the voodoo spell that took over their fearful bodies. They sat in silence as Agbenyaga tossed a magic potion of powders into the fire and watched an enormous red glow light up the sky. Faces of the past began to appear within the red glow above as Agbenyaga and her tribe began their spiritual chant.

The boys watched and listened to the cries of all the spirits in the sky as they desperately yearned for someone to save their souls.

"I'm scared," Billy whispered.

Something strange was happening, but the boys were unable to move. The drums began to get louder as the tribal warriors danced around the circle of fire. It was as if they were frozen in place, until the flames shot up toward the sky and turned into dying embers raining down upon the sand.

Suddenly, the voodoo spell lifted, and the boys slowly crawled backward away from the tribal ritual until they were safely out of sight.

Chapter 8

LUNCH TIME IN THE SCHOOLYARD the next day took a surprising turn when the big freckle-faced bully reached down into his school bag and pulled out an extra sandwich to share with Timmy. Inside the crinkled wax paper was a ham and cheese with pickle and mustard sandwich that looked like it had been thrown together in a hurry. Naturally, Timmy wondered if Billy had an ulterior motive or whether this was the olive branch he had been hoping for since the beginning of the school year. Just in case and to be on the safe side, he carefully examined the sandwich from top to bottom to make sure it wasn't another trick.

"Thanks, a whole bunch Billy. This is my favorite," he said finally, letting out a sigh of relief.

The children in the schoolyard began to whisper and wonder if the naive boy from the big city just became part of a more sinister plan to be recruited into Billy's gang. After all, no one ever survived the wrath of "Billy the Bully," no matter how hard they tried.

As soon as the students returned to their classrooms, an announcement of an early dismissal came over the loudspeaker. Immediately, the children switched into high gear and excitedly made plans for a free afternoon without any homework. Timmy made a mad dash toward the bus with Billy right behind him, to get his favorite seat behind the driver. As Timmy's foot hit the bottom of the step, Billy grabbed him from behind and pulled him so hard that he tumbled back off the bus steps. The bus driver was so busy speaking with the dispatcher that he didn't notice Billy pulling the door shut while Timmy was scrambling to get back on his feet. The sight of the city boy running behind the bus had Billy and his gang in hysterics, until the bus driver noticed his missing passenger in his side view mirror.

The bus came to an immediate stop so Timmy could climb aboard. As he walked down the aisle to find an empty seat, he wasn't at all surprised to find his number-one enemy pulling Joey Mather onto the floor so he could sit down in his seat.

The whole ride home, Timmy could hear Billy taunting the young boy. "Hold my books, you little twerp," he grumbled. Billy had an evil streak that just would not quit.

Joey sat on the floor of the bus, holding Billy's books while the rest of the gang made fun of him. A fit of anger came over Timmy as he marched down the aisle to pull Billy out of Joey Mather's seat.

"Sit back in your seat, Joey."

"But I'm scared."

"Hey! What's your deal? I thought we were friends," Billy said to Timmy in a threatening tone of voice.

"Leave Joey alone. He never did anything to you.

Joey wiped the tears from his eyes and sat back down as Timmy walked back to his seat in the middle of the bus. Within seconds, he could feel the hairs on the back of his neck stand at attention at the sound of heavy pounding footsteps getting closer toward his seat. Suddenly, the enemy tapped him on his shoulder and let out a warning that would put him in a tailspin.

"You better watch your back at school tomorrow, Timmy Boy, because when you least expect it, I'm going to clobber you."

At the next stop, Billy jumped off the bus and took off in the opposite direction. All the way home, Timmy couldn't help but wonder what terrible fate he would suffer at school the next day.

The night flew by so fast that he didn't even have time to prepare himself for the doom that awaited him that morning. All he could think about was that the master of trickery and deceit put a target on his back and was about to unleash his fury on him. His father sensed something was wrong and decided to secretly follow the bus to school.

The fear of facing Billy all alone grew stronger as the bus made its final turn into the school parking lot. As he inched his way off the seat, he could see a tall strong figure standing next to Billy, waiting patiently for the bus doors to open. It was Billy's father, whose face looked worn out from worry, as if he had just come back from a war. Timmy thought he would fall to his knees at any moment, but he remembered what Monty said about not showing your opponent that you are afraid. Instantly, he put on his game face and looked straight into the eyes of his archenemy. Just then, Michael appeared out of the shadows, slowly grasping Timmy by the arm as Timmy stepped down off the bus.

"What are you doing here, Dad?"

"I forgot to tell you something."

"What is it?"

"Battles are not meant to be fought alone."

The screeching sound of the bus doors closing behind them cut the tension between the two boys like a knife. Michael started to walk toward Billy's father and then stopped as he saw him begin to move. To their amazement, Billy's father stepped aside and there was Timmy's bike, painted back to its original color as if nothing had ever happened.

"Go ahead, Billy. Now you apologize and hand over his bicycle."

"I'm, uh, sorry for taking your bike and being so mean to you."

Michael reached out and shook hands with Joe, as men do when there is honor among them.

"My wife and I would love to have Billy stay over at our house this weekend," Michael said.

Timmy's stomach turned upside-down at the thought that pure evil was about to come and stay for a few days.

"I thought we were busy this weekend," Timmy said in a frantic tone of voice, looking anxiously up at his father.

"Now, son, this weekend will be just fine."

Timmy didn't buy it. The thought of sharing his home with the scariest boy in the neighborhood sent an overwhelming feeling of dread throughout his whole body. The weight of the world was heavier than he could ever imagine, and escape was impossible.

In a few short hours, the notorious Billy McDevitt would be standing outside his front door. The only thing he could do was to turn to the one place he felt safe, and that was inside the world of his comic book fantasies.

The uncomfortable feeling in the pit of his stomach grew stronger as Timmy waited for Billy to arrive. As he lay in his bed staring up at the ceiling, his heart pounded so hard he thought it would explode. Suddenly, the sound of the doorbell sent a chill clear through to his bones. He bolted down the stairway and stood directly behind his father, as if to shield himself from danger as his mother opened the door.

Chapter 9

THE PAIGE FAMILY HAD a night of pizza, popcorn, and movies planned, but before they could say a word, Monty jumped from the back of the chair right into Billy's arms. Billy looked like a bowl of Jell-O as he wobbled to his knees, holding onto Monty as if he had just caught the touchdown pass that won the game.

"This is one crazy cat," Billy blurted out.

"We found him outside, trapped under an old bicycle in that horrible storm," Monica replied.

"Come in and make yourself at home," Michael added.

Billy was on his best behavior, but Timmy knew all too well that he was putting on a show for his parents. His only defense was to be one step ahead of him if he wanted to survive the next forty-eight hours.

A shuffling sound came clear across the hardwood floors as the boys sat down in front of the fireplace. Jackie's comical entrance into the room holding her doll while wearing her mother's favorite shoes was another welcome distraction that seemed to tickle Billy's funny bone.

"Hi. My name is Jackie."

Billy looked down at Jackie and giggled as she began singing one of her favorite lullabies to anyone who would listen. A few minutes later, the doorbell rang again, but this time it was a pizza delivery man with a juicy, hot, oven-baked pizza with extra cheese.

"Pizza is my favorite," Billy commented.

"Mine too. Let's watch a movie."

"Your mom and dad are really cool."

"My dad is an architect."

"Boy, that's awesome. My dad is a retired ship captain who sailed all over the world."

"Did your dad ever see any pirates?"

"He used to tell me stories when I was little, but I don't remember now."

"Hey, I have an idea. Tomorrow, I can walk you home and we can ask your dad to tell us about all his adventures."

"Yeah. That sounds cool."

Suddenly, the sound of galloping paws came crashing through the room, sending the boys into a fit of laughter. Monty jumped over the loveseat and began running around in circles trying to catch his own tail. Jackie wiggled off the couch and ran after Monty as he darted out of the room and back up the stairs.

"Captain Hook is the coolest movie ever," Billy said as he reached for another piece of pizza.

"I can make you a sword out of newspaper if you want."

"Where did you learn how to do that?"

"My grandfather showed me last summer."

Timmy grabbed a few old papers from the trash bin and began showing Billy how to master the art of sword making out of a simple piece of paper. They even had a pretend sword fight before bedtime without any problems at all. Everything seemed too good to be true, leaving Timmy to wonder if this was just another one of Billy's twisted games. But he kept on being friendly.

"Wait until you see my bedroom. I have a lot of cool stuff," Timmy added.

"Awesome. Let's go," Billy responded as he hurried up the stairs.

Billy looked in amazement at Timmy's room. It was filled with comic books, games, and even had a bed shaped like a racecar.

"I wish I had a bed like that. You are so lucky. Oh boy! You have the Battleship game."

"We can play a game tomorrow if you want."

"Yeah! That would be awesome."

As Billy reached into his overnight bag to put on his pajamas, he could hear a rustling sound coming from inside the bedroom closet.

"Jackie, did you lock Monty in the closet again?" Timmy asked as Jackie skipped down the hall.

Timmy opened the closet door and ducked as Monty catapulted off the top shelf and landed right on the back of Billy's head. Billy let out a piercing scream and started running around the room, trying to free himself from the kitten's claws that were tangled up in his curly hair. A few moments later, Timmy's parents entered the room and told the boys it was time for lights out. Monica grabbed hold of Monty and released him from Billy's fiery orange wavy hair.

"C'mon, Monty. Leave the boys alone. Playtime is over," she said as she turned off the lights.

"Goodnight, Mom and Dad."

BILLY CLIMBED INTO the guest bed on the other side of the room but before he could say another word, Timmy had fallen asleep. Billy stared at the moon shining through the window trying desperately to drown out the sound of the clock ticking in the distance.

Finally, he began to drift in and out of sleep until unusual rumbling sounds echoed again from behind the closet door. He sat up in the bed with the covers over his head and whispered across the room.

"Timmy, wake up. I think there's a mouse inside your closet."

Suddenly, the closet door flew open and a shadowy figure walked out. At first, Billy thought that the full moon was playing tricks on him. He was sure it was little Monty prancing out of the closet, but then the shadow grew so big it reached the top of the ceiling. He was so scared that he rolled off the bed onto the floor and crawled under the bed.

The next thing he knew, a red glowing light began to slowly spread around the bed. He thought for sure he was about to be swallowed up like a mouse inside the belly of a snake. He finally mustered up enough courage to poke his head out from under the bed.

At the foot of the bed stood a huge black-and-gray- striped cat with long whiskers and bright green piercing eyes.

"Who are you?" Billy asked in a trembling but curious voice.

The ferocious looking cat stood with his bright red glowing paws on his hips and glared right through Billy as if he could see deep inside his soul.

"I am Monty the Magnificat at your service. I have been waiting patiently for your arrival, Billy."

"How do you know my name? I must be dreaming, because I'm not stupid. I know cats don't know how to talk," Billy said as he ducked back under the bed.

In an instant, Monty's claws snagged Billy and pulled him out and to his feet. "It's time for you to face the truth," he said.

"Wake up Timmy," Billy shouted as he struggled to get away.

"He can't hear you. No one can."

Monty's deep voice created such a vibration that the bedroom window flew open and cracked the glass. Billy tried to make a run for it again, but Monty grabbed him by his nightshirt and whisked him into the night sky. Billy covered his eyes with his hands, hoping to wake up from his horrible dream, but he was very afraid it wasn't a dream at all, and he was about to face the music.

"Open your eyes Billy."

Billy peeked through his fingers at the sight of the full moon disappearing behind a cloak of darkness that seemed to never end, until the silhouette of a familiar house caught his eye.

"Isn't that Joey Mather's house?"

The veil of darkened clouds around them began to swirl like a tornado, carrying Billy towards the steps of a school bus parked outside the Elementary school. He tried to pull away, but the force of the wind trapped his every move.

"Why am I here?" he cried.

Suddenly, he was startled by the taunting sound of someone in the back of the bus. He could clearly see himself pushing Joey to the floor and stealing his seat. Monty gently let go of Billy's hand and watched as the once-proud bully began to feel ashamed at what he had done to poor Joey Mather. He walked through the bus and approached the innocent, beaten-down little boy who wouldn't hurt a fly.

"I'm sorry, Joey. Come here and sit back down in your seat."

"He cannot see or hear you. It's time to go, Billy."

"Where are we going? I want to go home now. Please take me home now."

Once again, he began to feel the strength of the wind beneath his feet as Monty grabbed his hand. He turned around to take one last look, but the bus and Joey Mather had disappeared behind the swirling cloud. Billy wondered who and what was coming next.

"Are you hungry, Billy?"

"I guess so, but I wanna go back now."

Lunchtime in the schoolyard was his favorite time of day and the only place he felt in total control, but this time it was different. Monty let go of his hand and watched as Billy walked slowly through the schoolyard.

Over by the cherry tree, Billy could see his classmate Eddie Bowers sitting alone on an old tree stump, counting his allowance that he had saved for the last three weeks. Once again, Billy watched his past come to life before him. He tried to keep his eyes closed, but a force beyond his control held him captive and unable to move as he watched himself throw Eddie Bowers to the ground so he could pick through his pockets and steal his lunch money. Eddie just lay there, trying to gather the few pennies that Billy tossed at him as he left the scene of the crime.

"I feel really sick in my stomach," Billy whimpered.

"The only way to change for the better is to face what you have done," said Monty.

He could feel Eddie's hunger pains as if they were his own, and he began to see the horrible effect he had on the poor innocent boy that he tortured everyday just for the fun of it.

"Please! I didn't mean it."

"We are all responsible for our actions toward others Billy. It's time."

"Time for what? I thought you were taking me back now."

"There is one more stop we have to make, and this is the most important one of all."

They arrived at Julie Cooper's backyard birthday party. Monty explained that Julie had just moved to the neighborhood, and she had invited her whole class to her birthday celebration. Billy watched as Julie's parents scrambled to decorate the yard with streamers, balloons, games, a piñata full of goodies, and an inflatable swimming pool that would be perfect for a hot day in the sun. Her parents worked long into the night to complete the preparations for their daughter's birthday.

It was perfect. Perfect that is, until he could see someone sneaking into her backyard in the dark of night.

"Oh no, there's someone in the yard," he shouted as if someone would be able to hear. He continued to watch closely as the intruder began deflating the swimming pool, breaking the piñata, ripping down the streamers, and busting all the balloons. In a moment of confusion, he turned to Monty to tell him that there was no one named Julie in his class.

"Reach into your pocket, Billy."

Billy reached into his pocket and found an old picture of his grandparents holding hands with his dad when he was a young boy. Instantly, the figure in the picture became clearer, along with the frightful realization that it was his own father as a child hurting one of his own classmates. At that moment, Billy put his head down and reached for Monty's paw.

"Can we leave now?" Billy asked.

Magically, he found himself back in bed looking deep into Monty's green piercing eyes. Somehow, he knew it was time to make a change.

"Billy, you know what you must do tomorrow, my friend."

Chapter 10

ALL THROUGH THE NIGHT, Billy wrestled with his blanket until the warmth from the morning sun woke him up from his restless sleep.

"Hey, Billy, did you sleep all right last night?" Timmy asked as he finished making his bed.

Billy stood speechless with his hands shaking as he gathered his belongings from the bed.

"Let's go down-stairs, Timmy continued. "My Mom's making breakfast."

The shame of all his misdeeds grew stronger as Billy looked into the eyes of the family who had opened their doors and welcomed him into their home. He sat motionless at the breakfast table while the visions of all his victims raced through his mind, until Monty came to the rescue by jumping right into the popcorn bowl left over from the night before. With popcorn stuck to his tail, he spooked at the sight of his own shadow on the wall and escaped up the stairs.

Billy's laughter soon turned into an outcry for forgiveness as he looked across the table and shouted, "I'm sorry for being so mean. I just know everybody hates me."

"NO, THEY DON'T, SWEETHEART," Monica said in her sweet and gentle voice. While she tried to comfort him, Michael snuck into the kitchen and called Billy's father.

"Hello, Joe. Your son seems to be upset about something. He'd probably be happy to see you right now."

"I'll be right over."

"Now, Billy, everything is going to be fine," Monica said.

"But I've been stealing Timmy's lunch at school every day."

"Is that true, Timmy?"

"Well, um, I guess so."

"How can everyone be so nice to me after everything I did?" Billy was still sniffling.

"The most important thing is that you realize your mistake and you try to make things better," Michael added.

Just then, Billy's father walked in and put his arm around his son.

"That's right, Billy."

"But, Dad, why do I do these things?"

"I don't know why. I did it too when I was your age."

"I know, Dad. I saw you."

"What do you mean?"

Billy laid his head down on the table as Joe wiped away his tears.

"Son, you just have to reach deep inside your heart and be a better person. Your mother would be so proud of you. I know I am."

"Joe, why don't you sit down and have breakfast with us," Michael suggested as he reached for another blueberry muffin.

"Sit next to me, Dad," Billy said excitedly.

It didn't take long for Timmy to seize the moment and start sharing his stories of great adventure with his new audience.

"You have a wild imagination, young man," Joe said as he reached for the coffee creamer.

"That's my boy." Michael said with a smile.

Jackie slid down off her chair and tugged on Joe's key set that dangled from his belt.

"Do you like my new doll?" She sweetly asked Joe.

"Why yes I do. She is very pretty. Just like you."

Jackie skipped away smiling from ear to ear all the way into the kitchen.

"Why don't you both come back and join us for dinner?" Monica suggested.

"What do you say, Billy? Do you want to have dinner with the Paige family tonight?"

"I'll bring over the rocket I made from balsa wood and show Timmy how to launch it."

"Wow! That would be awesome. Hey, Dad, what's balsa wood?" Timmy asked.

"Well, I think it was used back in World War I as a substitute for cork. Isn't that right, Joe?"

"That's right. It's a lightweight wood that could be used for aircraft gliders because it could be bent into different shapes without losing its strength."

"That sounds so cool," Timmy said.

"Mommy, look! There's a whole bunch of people outside," Jackie said, pointing to the window.

As Joe opened the door to leave, he could see all his friends and neighbor's midway down the path toward the Paige property. Billy turned to say goodbye and noticed a red glow coming from the bedroom window on the second floor. The shadow of a huge cat caught his eye but vanished before he could utter a word.

"Dad. Did you see that glow upstairs?"

"Your imagination is running away with you, Billy. Let's get home. There are chores to be done."

Before they could take another step, the crowd entered the front gate and gathered around the hundred-year-old oak tree in the center of the property. The sight of all those familiar faces from Joe's past brought back dreadful memories of his mistreatment of them when he was a child. An overwhelming feeling of panic seemed to squeeze the life out of him until a comforting hand upon his shoulder gave him the courage to make amends.

His eyes welled up with tears when he realized it was his classmate Julie Patterson, whom he had bullied so many years ago. She reached up to wipe away the tears that slowly traveled down the side of his cheek.

"Joe, there is no need to shed a tear for something that happened a very long time ago."

He stood there in shame as she wrapped her arms around him and spoke the three most beautiful words anyone could have ever whispered in his ear. "I forgive you."

Suddenly, Monty came running out the front door heading toward the blackjack oak with a pair of red mittens dangling from his mouth. In the blink of an eye, an amazing red glow shot from the bay window and began spreading through the entire town. The boys stood spellbound as the power of the mystical force engulfed the Paige property and placed the townspeople in a trance-like state. The energy surrounding the historical mansion was so strong that the sky above them began to swirl like a raging fireball, pulling Monty like a magnet toward the edge of town.

"Hurry, Billy. We have to follow him."

"Ok. Let's get our bikes."

"What's going on, Michael?" Joe asked as they hurried into the old pickup.

"I don't know, but something tells me that we better catch up to the boys."

One by one, the townspeople began to follow the fiery red glow like they were following the Pied Piper of Hamlin toward the abandoned ships. Soon they poured through the entrance and made their way to the graveyard of unwanted ships.

While they stood there reminiscing about Black Sails Bay and its pirate past, the clouds above began to turn a dismal gray. Another storm carrying heavy gusts of wind was slowly moving along the coastal waterway and about to make landfall directly in the heart of Calico.

But before the storm could unleash its fury, Monty leaped onto one of the old ships and let out a feline cry that bellowed like thunder across the sky. Out of the blue, Agbenyaga, the high priestess of Yoruba, magically appeared in front of the boys and cast her spell of magic over the crowd.

"Do not be afraid," she said. "Only you and Billy can see me."

"Why are you here?" asked Timmy.

"I must help them remember the past or all the lost souls will vanish forever."

"What do you mean?" Billy replied with a confused look upon his face.

With piercing fire in her eyes, Agbenyaga raised her arms to the heavens and summoned the massive cargo ships that brought wealth and prosperity to their once- bustling town. The vision of ghostlike ships spread across the sky and stirred up memories of a town whose bay became a safe haven for seafaring vessels and their precious cargo. The boys listened closely to the crowd as they shared stories of famous ship captains who sailed along the Carolina coastal shores.

"I bet there are treasure chests full of pirate gold on these old ships," said Billy.

Timmy nodded. "I have an idea. I'll make a treasure map and meet you back here when the sun comes up to search for the gold."

As the boys tried to sneak in closer to the mysterious high priestess, she vanished into thin air, taking the ghostlike ships and the souls they carried with her. Meanwhile, Michael broke through the crowd as the people began to awaken from their mysterious spell and signaled to everyone to gather around.

"Join me on the mission to save this extraordinary place," Michael shouted as a bolt of lightning made its mark across the darkened sky.

But before they could discuss their plan, the powerful storm took a turn for the worse. Immediately, the women grabbed their children and headed for the safety of the nearby local church, while the men gathered to secure the man-made dam along the shoreline.

"Hurry! We don't have much time before the water reaches the dam," Michael shouted as he led all the men through the town.

Father Anthony greeted his congregation at the church and hurried the children down to the basement for safety. It didn't take long before a flash flood raced through the town heading straight toward nearby homes.

Chapter 11

THE TOWN OF CALICO was not prepared for the power behind the storm and had to adapt quickly. In an instant, the flood waters burst through the narrow end of the dam forcing them to fill the gap with heavy sandbags and redirect the flood away from the homes along the beach. But as they passed the sandbags down the line, the men could hear the screams of someone in trouble.

Michael led a small group of men swiftly toward the cries for help, only to find Joe and both the boys placing sandbags around the perimeter of the Nogo home. Daniel and Katherine Nogo were the first family to take up residence in Calico and the only surviving link to the

ancestry that symbolized the town and its history. They were proven descendants of slave families who had been separated and sold as property to work on nearby plantations before the turn of the fifteenth century. The couple often spent time at the local school, teaching the children about their family history and how their ancestors were some of the first to escape from slavery and live free in Calico.

Suddenly, the force of the flash flood broke a piece of the foundation loose, causing the Nogo home to partially collapse.

"Hurry, we haven't much time," one man shouted.

The men tried desperately to barricade the rest of the house against the force of the raging flood waters, but their attempts to secure the home became futile. The violent weather continued to challenge the men as they struggled to work with only the full moon to light their way.

The women set up a makeshift triage in the basement of the old church to care for any injured and to prepare hot food and drink for their husbands who worked tirelessly throughout the night. As the women were comforting Katherine, a bolt of lightning hit one of the support beams, trapping her husband Daniel beneath their home. When the news of the accident reached the church, Katherine grabbed the middle of her chest and stumbled.

As she tried to regain her balance, she gasped for air and spoke in a trembling voice. "I feel like something heavy is sitting on my chest."

Monica helped Katherine to her feet and took her across the overhead walkway to the nearby rectory. Katherine suffered from a weakened heart and someone needed to watch her throughout the night. As she lay resting in the private quarters of the church, she became curious about the Paige family and their interest in her small southern town.

"Tell me, dear," she said to Monica, what brought you and your lovely family to Calico?"

"My husband read an article about Black Sails Bay and thought he could help preserve its history."

"Oh! So, you are aware of our pirate past."

"My husband's fascination with pirates began as a child and continues to this day."

"Well. There are plenty of stories to be told. You will have to come by for some tea and I will share what I know to be true about the shipwreck pirates who landed here."

"That would be wonderful, but right now you need to get your rest, Katherine."

Monica spent the rest of the night at the bedside of her new neighbor, while Father Anthony addressed the rest of the congregation in prayer for Daniel's safe rescue.

Long hours without any sign of life coming from Daniel began to weigh on the shoulders of the men as they passed the last of the sandbags down the line. Time was running out for Daniel.

In the distance, the men could hear the pounding of drums coming from the high priestess, Agbenyaga, and her tribesman as they chanted to their voodoo gods throughout the night. Over time, Yoruba and its voodoo rituals became part of Calico folklore. But the boys' first-hand experience with Agbenyaga on the beach by the bay erased all doubt of her power within the spirit world.

"We better hurry before she turns us into stone," Billy muttered.

"No, silly, she's going to cast another spell," Timmy nervously replied. "My body is tingling all over," he added as he grabbed hold of Billy's raincoat.

"Oh boy! So is mine. What's going on?"

A fiery red hue began to glow across the sky, bringing a powerful warm burst of energy to the tired men who desperately needed to carry on with the rescue effort.

"Get the forklift out of the garage," Joe shouted as he struggled to clear away the broken beam.

The boys and two of the men battled against the wind and rain as they pulled themselves along the emergency rope line that was bolted to the garage. Finally, they reached the forklift that was secured with heavy chains to an old tractor inside against the wall.

Over the years, the garage had sustained water damage from a tree branch that had crashed through the roof above and rusted the antique iron padlock. The men failed at every attempt to remove the lock until Billy noticed an old oil can sitting on a crossbeam above his head.

He scrambled up to the top of the tractor and was able to reach the antique wooden handle that dangled from the side of the can.

"Oh no! It's empty." He threw the can across the room in frustration.

"We only need a few drops," Timmy said as he grabbed the can off the floor.

Every minute seemed like an hour as they patiently waited for a drop of oil to find its way to the tip of the oil can spout.

"Eureka!" one of the men shouted as drops of oil began dripping into the lock.

While the men removed the chains and drove the forklift to the house, the boys made their way back along the rope with extra supplies strapped to their backs. Upon their return, Father Anthony told them that all signs of life were gone, and any hope of saving Daniel may have been lost. Finally, the forklift was in place with Joe about to pull the levers into position.

"I don't know how much longer the support beam will hold," Joe said as he locked the controls into place.

A moment of silence spread throughout the group as they joined hands and bowed their heads for a quick prayer. Just then, one of the men came running from behind the house to tell everyone that he thought he heard faint sounds coming from under the house. This encouraged the men to work even harder to reach Daniel, whose life was truly in their hands. But each time they tried to raise the beam; the wheels of the forklift began to slide backward.

"Get those bricks and brace the wheels," one of the men shouted.

The boys joined the men and passed down brick after brick until a wall of weight sat firmly behind the forklift.

"We need to get back to the triage and come up with a plan. I am going to need one of you to stay behind with Dan and keep him talking," Michael shouted with a deep sense of despair.

"I'll keep an eye on things here. Just bring me back a hot cup of cocoa," Joe replied.

While the men were working out how to free Daniel, Joe thought he heard distinct tapping sounds coming more frequently from under the house. He quickly followed the sound and crawled alongside the house until a glimmer of hope caught his eye. It was Daniels antique shiny silver medallion that Katherine had custom made for him for their twenty-fifth wedding anniversary.

"Save yourself, Joe, and tell Katherine I love her with all my heart," Daniel said weakly.

"You are not going to give up now, not on my watch," Joe said firmly.

Moments later, the men returned and found Joe had jammed a piece of wood behind the lever of the forklift and crawled under the house in a final attempt to reach Daniel. Everyone sprang into action and started scooping out the softened mud with their bare hands while Joe crawled as close as he could to Daniel. He was able to grab hold of Daniel's thick leather belt, and he pulled as hard as he could until the force of the flood water pushed Daniel's body close enough for the men to drag him out from under the house. But just as Joe began to crawl out, the splintered beam split in half and fell, pinning his back and legs underneath the house.

"Hurry! We have to dig Joe out," Michael screamed as the boys ran toward the forklift to try and help.

"Timmy. Help me up to the seat," Billy said.

"Do you know how to work the controls?"

"Yeah. My dad used to let me practice all the time."

Timmy cupped his hands together and hoisted Billy onto the seat. He sat behind the controls of the forklift and managed to lift the corner of the house high enough for the men to place heavy cinder blocks on top of each other underneath the house. The men furiously dug out the softened mud on each side of Joe and slid him out before the bricks gave way.

"I need two men at his shoulders, two at his hips, and the boys can grab his legs. On the count of three, we lift him up and lay him on the sandbags next to Daniel until help can arrive," Michael shouted.

Daniel was moaning in pain from his fractured ribs, but alert enough to reach his hand out to Joe.

"You saved my life, Joe. How can I ever thank you?" said Daniel in a weak and trembling voice.

"Look everybody! someone yelled. "The floodwaters are receding."

"I was able to get an emergency call through to the heliport at Mercy General," another man shouted.

Finally, the ferocious storm began to slowly calm, and the sun came over the horizon.

"Where did that red glow come from?" Daniel asked.

Joe signaled for the men to lean down and listen to his painful whisper. "The answer can be found in the manifest deep inside the tunnel."

Michael believed Joe's feverish words to be caused by his confused state of mind due to his injuries, but a group of men were huddled in the corner questioning whether there could be some truth to what Joe was saying about a hidden manifest. Afterall, no one could explain the mysterious red hue that lit up the sky during the rescue. In the distance, the boys could hear the medevac helicopter approaching the washed-out road in front of the house.

"Ok Boys. Hurry over to the church and tell Father Anthony we're on our way," Michael shouted.

As soon as the injured were airlifted to the hospital, the men returned to the church to enjoy a happy reunion with their loved ones. Father Anthony blessed all those who braved the storm, then he joined the men in a hearty feast prepared by his congregation.

Chapter 12

OVER THE NEXT FEW MONTHS, every child in town volunteered all their spare time to the ongoing cleanup efforts down at the bay. This labor of love continued from sunup to sundown during Joe McDevitt's intense six-month rehabilitation program.

The final week was going according to plan until one afternoon, when another intense cold front along the coastal waters forced the boys to head home sooner than expected.

"Hey, Timmy. Your whole face is as red as a cherry," laughed Billy as they hurried home to change into warmer clothing.

"When do you think your dad will be coming home?"

"I hope soon. I really miss him."

"I better get home for dinner. Do you want to come over?"

"No, I have to call the hospital and check in with my neighbors who are keeping an eye on me until my dad gets home."

As Billy briskly walked on the winding pebble road, he thought he saw someone in the window of the private study but before he could look more closely, a rabbit jumping out of a metal trash bin startled him into looking away from the house. When he looked up at the house again, the image was gone, leaving him to wonder if he was imagining things. After all, he was exhausted from putting in a long hard day of work down at the bay.

A piece of bright yellow paper was dangling from the front door of the house. He quickly ripped the note off the door and went inside to sit down in his father's favorite rocking chair. The exciting news that his father would be released the next morning brought tears to his eyes and motivated him to clean up the house before his father's return. In haste, he systematically went from room to room putting everything in its place until he fell asleep at the kitchen table, right in the middle of drinking a cold glass of farmer's milk.

Bright and early the next morning, the sound of birds chirping stirred him from his slumber. As he looked out the kitchen window at his father's old pickup, he realized that his practice days were over and that he would have to drive the truck on his own for the first time.

He began his first attempt at being a grownup by reaching into the cupboard for his father's favorite coffee beans and making a fresh pot of coffee. The scent of the coffee brewing early in the morning seemed to give him a sense of confidence, especially as he was about to make his first step into adulthood. Although he wasn't of age, his father felt it was important to teach his son to be self-sufficient by allowing him to drive the truck short distances in case an emergency ever arose. With a deep breath and his head held high, Billy poured his first cup of coffee and placed a call to his father's hospital room.

"Hello," Joe said in a painful whisper.

"Dad, I'm going to pick you up this morning."

"Be careful. I know you'll do just fine."

"Thanks. See you later."

Billy grabbed the keys off the key rack, started up the pickup, and headed down the back roads to the hospital. The serpentine road that led from his house and into town became difficult at every turn, but he proved himself able to master the challenge in front of him.

The hospital nurse stood next to Joe as he sat patiently in his wheelchair looking out his hospital window for his son to arrive. A smile formed at the corner of his mouth as he watched his truck turn onto the main road leading to the front of Mercy General Trauma Center. Billy parked the truck right in front of the hospital entrance and rushed in to wait for the next elevator. The day was finally here, and to show his gratitude, Billy had picked up a basket of freshly baked muffins along the way. He gave it to the nurse who monitored his father's care.

"Help me put my shoes on, Billy."

He gathered his father's belongings while the nurse went over the discharge instructions given to patients who were ready to manage their own care at home.

Unfortunately, Joe's injuries left him with a permanent limp, but otherwise he would remain as whole as a man could hope for under the circumstances. Billy followed as the nurse pushed his father in a wheelchair down the long hallway to the elevator doors. Joe let out a sigh of relief as the elevator descended to the main floor of the hospital. As the doors opened, he reached behind his left shoulder and grasped the nurse's hand.

"Please tell everyone how grateful I am to have had such a wonderful medical team taking such good care of me."

The nurse smiled and waved goodbye at the archway of the waiting room. Joe rose up out of his seat with the help of his cane and held on to Billy as they walked carefully out of the hospital and over to the truck. Despite the struggle, he was able to use the truck step and spring up onto the front passenger seat with hardly any help at all. He looked over at his son and said, "You're a pretty good driver."

"Do you mean it?"

"Your old man isn't a bad teacher after all. Well, son, start her up."

As Billy carefully pulled out in the direction of the main road, he noticed a large group of balloons floating up in the air ahead of him.

"What's happening? There are people everywhere. It looks like a celebration is going on in town."

The sound of laughter and cheers echoed through the air as he drove the old pickup closer to the center of town. Billy had no idea that the news of his father's release from the hospital had spread so quickly.

The residents of Calico had decorated every storefront with colorful streamers and banners in celebration of Joe's return. A short distance away, they could see a large table set with a feast fit for a king outside the general store. Billy pulled up and parked the truck right on the side of the road. Katherine and Daniel greeted them with a barrel of fresh fruits and vegetables from their garden, along with her first-place Blue Ribbon home-baked apple pie. The overwhelming response from their neighbors brought tears to their eyes as they sat down to celebrate with all their new friends. Daniel stood up from the table and raised his glass. "I don't know how I will ever repay you for saving my life, Joe."

"I can't take all the credit. I couldn't have done it without the help of my good friends and neighbors. Thank you all for welcoming me home in such a wonderful way."

As time passed, Joe became noticeably tired from all the excitement and waved goodbye to everyone. He welcomed the short ride home and was relieved to soon be sitting in his favorite rocking chair in the study. Joe smiled and pulled the blanket over his legs while Billy went into the kitchen to get dessert.

"There's nothing like a home-baked apple pie to make all your problems go away," Joe said with a smile.

"You said it, Pop!" Billy replied.

He poured two glasses of fresh farmer's milk and warmed up the blue-ribbon apple pie. It didn't take long before their pieces were reduced to a few crumbs on the plate.

"Ok, Billy, it's time we both got a good night's sleep."

Early the next morning, Billy gathered all the fresh vegetables from Katherine and Daniel's basket and surprised his father with a hearty breakfast. The smell of a fresh pot of coffee lingered in the air as Joe hobbled into the kitchen. In the center of the table was an enormous homemade omelet with fresh cut ham, cheese, and vegetables waiting to be enjoyed. It was piping hot and ready to eat with homemade biscuits and fresh pastries for dessert.

"I didn't know you could cook."

"I found Mom's old recipe book in the kitchen drawer."

"You know how much your mother enjoyed eating breakfast together. Thank you, son."

"I can feel her all around us."

"I feel her too. You took on all the responsibility as man of the house while I was away. I'm so proud of you, son."

"Thanks, Dad."

"I overheard the nurses talking about all the hard work being done to clean up the bay."

"Me and my friends have been working with Timmy's dad every day while you were in the hospital."

Suddenly, the sound of the telephone ringing in the hallway interrupted their conversation.

Billy ran to answer the phone. "Hi Mr. Paige."

"Hi, Billy. I just wanted to let you know that I won't be needing you today. I want you to stay home and take care of your dad. See you tomorrow."

"Hey, Dad! Mr. Paige said he doesn't need me today."

"I guess it's just you and me then. We have a lot of catching up to do. It sure is good to be home."

Back at the shipyard, an intriguing story began to unfold as Michael searched through the hull of the last remaining ship to dock at the bay. On the bridge of the ship he accidently stumbled upon an old chest that held the captain's personal ledger hidden among the nautical charts. Immediately, he left for home to share the news with his wife who was assisting him with documenting the contents left behind by the infamous pirates who sailed the Carolina Coast. He burst through the front door with the ledger and nautical maps grasped in his hands just as his wife was setting the table for dinner.

"WHERE ARE THE CHILDREN? You're not going to believe what I found."

"They're upstairs in their rooms. What have you got there?"

"It's a cargo manifest, and it just might be the last documentation left behind by the captain's first mate."

"How about we look at it later when the children go to bed?"

"You're right. It has been a long day. I'll let the children know it's time for dinner."

The family caught up on the day's events. Michael welcomed the distraction, especially his daughter's surprise of a homemade vanilla pudding with fresh blueberries and whipped cream that she helped make that afternoon.

"This is the best dessert I ever had, Jackie."

"Me and Mommy had so much fun and I even licked the spoon too."

"Can I have some more pudding, Mom?" Timmy asked before he'd even finished gobbling up his last spoonful of dessert.

Everyone had seconds of her delicious, sweet treat and then headed to the living room to play board games until it was time to turn in for the night. As the children lay snuggled in their beds, Michael read the detailed ledger to his wife. It explained the existence of courthouse documents that would reveal an inhumane way of life that was a common practice among the affluent society of that time.

The rich used their power to buy the sweat and tears of the poor for their own personal gain by supplying marginal food, shelter, and the promise of a better life to all those who lived in poverty. These documents will prove that all slaves were the property of their masters and lived a life of grueling back-breaking work, often in dangerously high temperatures, without any regard for their health and well-being. Their only hope of freedom lay in the hands of a few good men and women who sacrificed their lives to rescue those unfortunate people.

"This confirms Black Sails Bay played a vital role in harboring slaves who fled from their wealthy plantation owners back in the seventeen hundred," said Michael looking up from the ledger at Monica.

"When I was taking care of Katherine at the church, she mentioned that she knew the history surrounding the pirates who docked at Black Sails Bay. She told me to come by for some tea and she would tell me all about her ancestors who were enslaved by the plantation owners you mentioned. There's more to this story than meets the eye Michael," Monica said.

"There has to be more information on those old ships. If Katherine's ancestors worked on those plantations, then we need to uncover the truth of what happened to all those people who worked the fields during that time. I want to stop and check in with Joe before I head to the shipyard tomorrow morning," Michael replied.

"I have a strange feeling that Katherine may have more information about the underground railroad formed in the late 1700s. I read an article about how those secret routes helped the slaves escape into free states. I'll make a fresh batch of blueberry muffins for you to take to Joe," said Monica as she entered the kitchen.

"I think Daniel will have more information to add to her story. I want to put this manifest in a safe place," said Michael as he hurried up the stairs.

While Monica was whipping up her family favorite recipe for blueberry muffins, the curiosity surrounding Joe's ancestry consumed Michael's attention. He sat on the end of his bed and reread the manifest wondering what secrets he will uncover down at the shipyard. As soon as he finished reading the last entry of the manifest, he carefully secured it in an old trunk in the back of his bedroom closet.

Chapter 13

BRIGHT AND EARLY THE next morning, a cluster of broadcast media personnel gathered on the front lawn of the McDevitt house. News had spread, bringing reporters from neighboring counties to interview the town hero, but Joe had a better idea. He sent them over to the courthouse to find his friend Michael Paige who was supervising the restoration of Calico's historical landmark. Moments later, Billy helped his father back to bed and snuck out to meet with his friends at their favorite hideout at the edge of town.

A few hours into his sleep, Joe was awakened by an enormous crash from the downstairs library. As he hobbled over to look out his bedroom door, a shadowy figure appeared midway down his stairwell.

"Who are you?" Joe demanded as he shook his cane at the intruder.

A strange feeling came over his whole body and he was eerily drawn to follow the apparition. The bearded man was dressed in brightly colored, mismatched loose clothing, and he held a black and gray striped tabby cat in his arms. The smell of the salty sea air surrounded the figure as Joe followed him down the stairway and into the library. As a child, Joe had found a picture of a pirate hidden between the pages of an old book given to him by his father on his thirteenth birthday. This old pirate looked somewhat similar, and he wondered if he could be that same man as in his picture. Before Joe's foot touched down on the last step, the mysterious pirate pointed to the portrait that had fallen to the floor and instantly vanished before Joe could utter a word.

The room was extremely cold despite the 100-degree temperature outside, leaving Joe to wonder if his fever had returned. Before he could put all the pieces together and come up with a reasonable explanation, an unexpected knock at the door startled him. He pulled the curtain away from the window to see Michael standing patiently on his doorstep with a basket of freshly baked muffins.

"Come in, Michael. The door is unlocked. A group of reporters were on my lawn first thing this morning. I sent them down to the courthouse to interview you about the project."

"Are you all right? You look like you've seen a ghost."

Joe wiped his sweat-beaded brow and pointed his cane toward the library. As Michael poked his head into the room, he noticed the portrait lying on the floor surrounded by a pool of water. The air smelled of the sea.

"What happened in here?"

"Would you mind helping me put this picture back where it belongs?"

***

Michael carefully began to pick up the portrait of Joe's ancestor when suddenly, the old brick wall where the picture once hung began to move to one side. They both took a sharp step back and found themselves staring into a dark and unknown place hidden deep behind the library walls.

"It's a tunnel," Joe said with a quiver in his voice.

"I think you should wait here Joe, while I take a look. Do you have a flashlight?"

"I think there is one in the desk, but the batteries are old. Why don't you use the candle instead? Something tells me I better come along," Joe said in a curious tone.

A rush of adrenaline flowed through Joe's body as he followed closely behind Michael. He was unafraid and eager to discover where the tunnel would take him. The glow from the candle illuminated the narrow passageway as Michael led the way deeper into the darkness. A quarter mile into their journey, they noticed scraps of old clothing scattered about the entrance to a secret room.

"What is this place? There are tunnels going in every direction," Michael said.

In the corner of the room was a table carved out of an old tree stump, and in the middle of the table was an aged and weathered manifest. Michael wiped away the dust and dirt and began to read detailed descriptions of a cargo that was transported by ship and considered not only against the law back at the turn of the century, but punishable by hanging.

"I think these tunnels were used as a safe passage for slaves. This is the missing link to what I found in a cargo manifest down at the shipyard," Michael said as he picked up an old oil lamp lying on the dirt floor. He carefully brushed away the cobwebs and lit the end of the wick.

"Blow out your candle, Joe. When the wick goes out, we can use the candle to light our way back."

"Good idea. But what are those markings on the wall?"

Michael waved the oil lamp along the wall and could not believe his eyes.

"Look! These names could be some of the slaves who escaped through here."

"They didn't want to be forgotten," Joe shakily replied.

As they walked farther into the tunnel, the flame of the cracked oil lamp began to dance to a cold breeze coming from the earth above. Michael began to break through the twisted branches that blocked their way and found an old thick mooring line partially embedded in the dirt.

"It's a ladder. I bet this was used to help the slaves climb down and hide from their captors."

The excitement overwhelmed Joe so much that he forgot all about his injuries and climbed up the ladder without any assistance. As soon as he pushed through the debris, he realized he was right in the galley of one of the old abandoned ships.

"I feel stronger than I have in months. Look! There's a big tabby cat lying on top of the stove."

He walked over to pet the cat and realized she was a bit frail. Michael came over to check and noticed a strange red powder on the tabby's underbelly and paws.

"That's odd. My kitten Monty had that same stuff on his belly when we found him."

"I better take her back to the house to give her something to eat," Joe replied.

Joe searched the ship for an empty crate as Michael sat down on an old barrel and began to read the pages of the manifest.

"Wait! Listen to this, Joe. It's incredible. Your family tree dates back to the late seventeen hundred, and you're the direct descendant of Captain Jack McDevitt, also known as "The Hawk" who was accused of providing slaves safe passage away from plantation owners. Captain Jack became a fearless fighter against the idea that one human being could become the property of another. The proof is all here, Joe. It says that in the dead of night, Captain Jack would sail along the riverbank and rescue any lost soul who dared to escape their captors."

"My father would spin tall tales about a famous pirate who lived right here in Calico, but I was so young that I didn't truly understand it all. Come on, we better get back now."

They climbed down the ladder and retraced their steps back to the hidden room, the crate with the cat safely in Michael's arms. As they reached the end of the tunnel, they were surprised to find Billy standing there waiting for them.

"Hi Mr. Paige. Hey, Dad, what is this place? And where did you find that cat?"

"Inside the galley of one of the old ships. She even has stuff on her belly like Monty."

"Do you think this could be Monty's mother?" Billy asked. Billy slowly spun around in a circle; his eyes fixed on the tunnels underneath his house. "I have to call Timmy right away and tell him all about this place."

Billy left the hidden room with his father right behind him and headed for the library to call his friend. But before he could make the call, his father grabbed the receiver out of his hand.

"No, Billy. We mustn't tell anyone until we find out what really happened so long ago."

"Your father is right," said Michael. "Until we get all the facts, we must protect your family ancestry."

"But what about Timmy?"

"You were man enough to drive the pickup, and now you must be man enough to keep our secret."

"Hey, Dad! This would make me your first mate. Right?"

Joe and Michael looked at each other and immediately stood at attention to give Billy a formal salute.

"Protect our secret until further orders," both men shouted.

"Aye, aye, Captain," Billy replied in his best pirate voice.

Joe and Michael smiled at each other as Billy picked up the tabby cat and took her into the kitchen. "I think she's scared and hungry, Pop. I'm going to get her a bowl of cold milk."

An amazing tale began to unfold as Michael read the true story of how two friends joined together to change a great injustice that preyed on the poor and innocent. The manifest brought to light the bravery of a single slave named Jon "Mock" Masterson who traveled to free Captain Jack from a fate worse than death. It happened one stormy night when the river began to rise so fast that it spun the boat around until it crashed against the rocky riverbank. Captain Jack was knocked unconscious and captured by Thomas W. Grant, the owner of one of the largest plantations in South Carolina.

The next morning, he was transported to a nearby island known for selling slaves to the highest bidder. He was held captive for several months until Mock Masterson risked his life to help Captain Jack escape the same torture that he once endured on what was known as the Island of Doom.

On that fateful night, Captain Jack chose Mock Masterson as second-in-command, and as they floated down river under the brilliant light of the moon, both men made a pact to embark on a lifelong quest to set free all who fell victim to a life of abuse at the hands of the rich and powerful.

"Do you mind if I share this incredible discovery?"

Joe looked up at Michael with a tear in his eye and said, "I believe Captain Jack and Mock Masterson would want their story shared with the rest of the world."

"Could you ever have imagined that your family would play such an important role in history?" said Michael as he helped Joe into the study.

"I am so happy to know that my family was instrumental in helping all those poor souls," said Joe as he wiped the sweat off his brow.

Michael wrapped the manifest in an old cotton cleaning cloth and rushed home to share the incredible news with his wife.

Chapter 14

THE SOUND OF THE KEYS in the door in the middle of the afternoon startled Monica. After all, Michael wasn't due home for a few more hours. The look on his face spoke volumes as he rushed into the living room.

"Oh! You're home early," Monica said. "How is Joe doing?"

"He's still on the mend, but every day he's getting better. Honey, you're not going to believe the story I'm about to tell you. I think you better sit down."

His wife listened intently as Michael described how the McDevitt family was directly descended from a pirate turned liberator who provided freedom to hundreds of slaves forced to live a life of hard labor.

"I never thought in my wildest dreams that this town would have such an amazing secret. What are you going to do with all this information?" Monica asked.

"Joe gave me the green light to document the historical significance of his family legacy and present it to the head of the Historical Society."

"Just think, Michael, if you had never read that article about Black Sails Bay, this story may have been buried forever. It's our destiny, isn't it?"

"Yes. I believe it is."

Early the next morning, Michael drove his son through the quiet streets of Calico toward the Chamber of Commerce, located in the center of town.

"Can I get a pastry puff and chocolate milk?" Timmy asked hopefully.

"Sure. Let's bring some pastry to the board members to have with their morning coffee. But let's hurry."

Thankfully, a few board members were running late, giving Michael an opportunity to submit the manifest for review before the first order of business for the day.

"Good morning, Michael. How is the restoration going down at Black Sails Bay?" Robert Brock, President of the Architectural Society and head of the Historical Society glanced at Timmy and smiled.

"It's going well, but I'm here on another matter. I have in my hand a manifest that dates back to the seventeen hundred, and inside is information proving the bravery of two men from Calico: Captain Jack McDevitt and his second-in-command, Jon "Mock" Masterson, who risked their lives to free slaves.

"Oh boy! A real-life pirate lived in Billy's house," Timmy blurted out.

"Young man, I want you to wait in the hall until your dad returns," said Robert Brock as Timmy left the room.

"Are you saying that Joe McDevitt's family fought against the practice of slavery? Come with me and you can present the facts to our board members before the meeting."

The greatest story ever to be found in the quiet little town began to unravel as Michael read page after page of the major events that took place in Calico hundreds of years before.

"Listen to this passage from Captain Jack himself. 'One dark night along the outer banks of the Black River, the spirit world entered the soul of Mock and his trusty tabby cat Montego. As he sat gazing into the eternal flame, he reached into his pouch of magic powders and sprinkled it over the fire. I watched as the potion sparked a red blistering fireball that shot out from the center of the cave. A bright light took over Jon Masterson's body as he walked toward the ocean's edge and spoke aloud for everyone to hear. "Do not be afraid. I have called upon the spirits in the sky to light the way this very night and all those who believe will be set free."

'This bright red glow would send a message across the sky telling every man, woman, and child that on that chosen night many slaves would be saved. The powerful energy released by this mystical glow would summon the inner strength of anyone whose spirit was weakened by the torture and daily strife of indentured servitude.

'On this night, we began our quest to free our brothers and sisters from the chains that bound their souls." Captain Jack's signature and the date of 1742 is right here for all the world to see."

"This is an incredible discovery, my friend. Where did you find the manifest?" Robert asked.

"In a hidden tunnel underneath the McDevitt home. Come with me and I'll walk you through the tunnel that leads to the old ship. But I better call ahead to see if Joe is up for a visit."

Joe and Billy stood patiently on the front porch waiting for Robert Brock to arrive.

"This is the coolest thing ever, Pop."

"Make no mistake, son. Captain Jack was a very courageous man. Everyone will soon hear about a true hero who once lived in our town.

"I hope someday when I grow up, I can be just like Captain Jack. Look! I can see them coming over the hill, and Timmy is there too."

"Why don't you make some lunch for us while I take them through the underground cave, and did you remember the flashlight?"

"I gave it to Mr. Paige. Oh boy! I can't wait to tell Timmy all about the secret tunnels under our house."

Joe and Robert followed Michael through the cave to the hidden room. Robert pulled out his camera and began taking pictures as they entered the tunnel leading to the ship.

"These pictures will provide valuable data that will prove beyond a reasonable doubt that the McDevitt family was instrumental in changing the course of history in a significant way," Robert mentioned as he snapped a group of photos.

Robert glanced at Joe. "Are you feeling alright, Joe?" he asked.

"I am feeling a bit tired. Michael, why don't you take Robert the rest of the way and I'll see you when you get back."

Robert listened intently as Michael explained how Captain Jack and his first mate, Mock, used the ship as an escape route to sneak the slaves aboard in the dead of night and move them underground to safety. He pulled out a pad and pencil and began taking notes to develop the story for the local newspaper.

In his early years, Robert Brock began his career as an investigative reporter, which led to his relocation to Calico where he began a series of stories about the folklore of piracy known to be associated with the seafaring town. Over time, Robert Brock became deeply involved in documenting the history of Calico and was elected to maintain its vital records. After an hour of searching the ship and revisiting the hidden room, he had enough information to compile a story that would attract

the attention of not only Calico, but the local news media. As the men made their way back to the library, Joe headed to the kitchen where he could hear the boys pretending to be pirates heavily engaged in battle.

"Arrr, me bucko. It's time to walk the plank."

"Aye, aye, ya scurvy scallywag."

"Ok, boys. Let's finish up in the kitchen. It's time for lunch," Joe said, chuckling under his breath.

Billy scrambled for a seat at the table closest to his father as Joe pulled out old pictures from the family photo album and began sharing fragments of various stories he had heard as a child. Between mouthfuls, Robert jotted down specific details that he would later add to his story.

"Well, Joe. I think I have enough information to take back to the board members."

"Ok. Timmy, your mother must be wondering where you are."

Soon after, society members voted to host an enormous celebration at the town hall where Billy would accept an award of bravery on behalf of his now - favorite relative, Captain Jack McDevitt, alias "The Hawk" and Jon "Mock" Masterson, his loyal and trusted friend.

The morning of the celebration had Billy in a panic as he stood at his bedroom window trying to unscramble the jumbled thoughts in his head. He was about to go on stage and stand in front of the whole town and he was afraid. He quickly put on his Sunday best and ran down to the kitchen to make a pot of coffee for his dad.

To Billy's surprise, Joe was already sitting at the table with a hot cup of coffee and a basket of muffins left on the front porch by their neighbor across the road.

"Grab yourself a glass of milk, son, and come sit down with me," Joe said.

"Banana nut muffins are my favorite."

"I have a confession to make. They're my favorite too. So, today is a big day. Are you ready?"

"Yes, sir." Billy replied as he swallowed the last bite of his muffin.

"Well, let's get going then. Michael is driving us to the town hall."

On the way into town, the nervous tension between the boys reached its breaking point and erupted into an arm-wrestle challenge in the back seat.

"It looks like the boys are letting off some steam," Joe remarked.

The boys held their positions for as long as they could, but no matter how hard they tried, no one was going to win the bout. Billy became very quiet as they pulled around to the back of the town hall.

"I never saw so many people before," he said with a tremble in his voice.

The boys jumped out of the car and raced through to the backstage of the hall, where Jackie and Monica were waiting to give moral support to Billy before he walked out on to the stage.

The attendance at the ceremony was beyond everyone's expectations. The media coverage had captivated historians around the world who arrived to pay tribute to Calico's unsung heroes. Robert stepped up to the podium and welcomed everyone to the ceremony, while Billy and his father waited in the wings.

The story of Captain Jack and Jon "Mock" Masterson mesmerized the crowd as they listened intently to the detailed description of the secret underground tunnels that became the only way of escape for people who were bought, sold and forced to become the property of another. There was not a sound in the room as Billy peeked out from behind the curtains.

"I'm scared, Pop."

"Don't be. Somehow, I know Captain Jack is watching over you, son."

Billy took a deep breath and walked onto the stage, completely lost in the eyes of all his classmates who were standing in the front row. As he looked around the room at all the familiar faces before him, a bundle of words came jumping off his tongue.

"I'm sorry for being so mean to everybody," he said as he stood, frightened, in front of the crowded room.

Joe came out from behind the stage and placed his arm around his son's shoulder. "It's all right, son, go on."

Billy's hand was shaking as he reached down into his pocket and pulled out a crumpled piece of paper. He smoothed it out as best he could and started to read.

"I am so proud to know that Captain Jack is part of my family and that he was able to help so many people long ago. I hope someday that I can be just like him. I want to share this award with all my friends. Is that ok, Pop?"

The crowd began to roar as his classmates came forward to join him and his father on the stage. As the applause slowed down and just a few whispers remained, he raised the award above his head and led the crowd back through the town toward the bay where the festivities were ready to begin. The entire ship was decorated from the bow to the stern and filled with enough food and drink to feed an army. The rest of the day was spent celebrating and remembering all those who found refuge in their small Carolina town.

Sometime later, the media packed up to leave and the celebration came to an end. As Billy stood role-playing at the helm of the ship, he heard a group of boys fighting on the deck below over a pair of roller skates.

"Hey! Stop fighting. Meet me at the schoolyard in fifteen minutes. One of you can borrow my brand-new pair of skates."

The boys climbed down the ladder and ran toward the schoolyard to wait for Billy. In all the excitement, he didn't realize that his father had already left for home with the Paige family. He quickly said his goodbyes to the few remaining council members and left the shipyard to check in on his father.

Joe was sitting in his favorite rocking chair with a hot cup of cocoa topped with whipped cream as Billy barreled through the front door.

"I see you made it home all right," Joe said.

"Sorry, Dad. I was having so much fun with all my friends. Are you ok?"

"Just tired."

Billy placed the plaque on top of the fireplace mantel and ran up to his bedroom to grab his skates out from under his bed.

"Where are you going?" said Joe as he watched his son run up to his room.

"I promised to lend my new skates to one of my friends. They're waiting for me down at the schoolyard."

"You better hurry. It's starting to get dark."

Billy jumped on his skateboard and raced through several long blocks until he reached the schoolyard. He waited anxiously for the boys by the cherry tree until the sun began to go down, but no one ever showed. As he turned to walk away, the loose pebbles on the ground began to bounce like Mexican jumping beans, making it difficult for him to keep his balance. Was it an earthquake? He helplessly swayed from side to side until the mysterious high priestess Agbenyaga appeared in front of him like a cobra dancing to a snake charmer's flute.

Agbenyaga circled around him performing her familiar chant, while Billy covered his eyes in fear. Suddenly, the high priestess peeled his clenched hands from his eyes and spoke aloud.

"Come with me and do not be afraid."

"Where are we going?"

"It's time to save the lost souls and bring them home where they belong."

The high priestess grabbed hold of his hand and led him toward the beach where he could see the shadowy figure of a man walking along the water's edge. In the blink of an eye, the high priestess vanished into thin air, leaving him all alone with the mysterious stranger.

As he stood watching, Billy felt drawn to follow the bearded man along the beach until he disappeared in the heavy fog that rolled in off the ocean. "Where did he go? and what did he want?" he thought to himself.

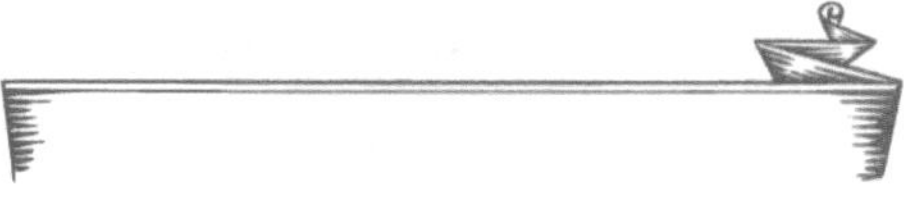

Chapter 15

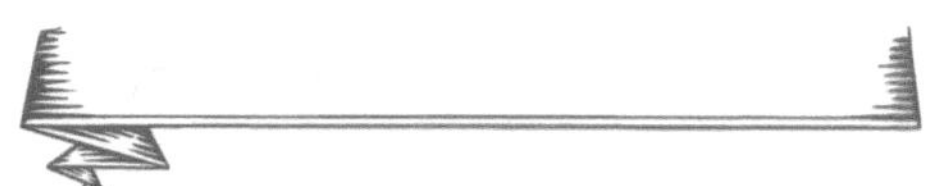

SOON, THE FOG BEGAN to clear, and he found himself standing in front of a huge wall of earth and rock covered in twisted seaweed. As he ripped through the thick and slimy branches, he uncovered a hollow opening that led him inside the mountain.

Fear mixed with the thrill of being inside the cave that Captain Jack had described in his manifest sent Billy running deeper into the underground chamber. An old pirate sword leaning against a pile of petrified wood caught his eye as he moved in closer to a makeshift fire pit nearby. He noticed the mishmash of old wine bottles and drinking mugs left behind by buccaneers and realized that the bearded man was the spirit of Captain Jack McDevitt.

Billy picked up the sword and began to swing it through the air as if he were in battle against the enemy, but as he was leaping around the cave, his foot hit against something buried in the ground. He leaned down and dug his fingers into the mix of sand and clay until a shiny object appeared. It was an ancient gold coin sitting there waiting for someone to come along.

"Finders, keepers," he shouted as he tucked the coin safely into his pocket.

A cool breeze brushed against his cheek and as if someone guided his hand, he grabbed one of the mugs and began singing, "Yo! Ho! Yo! Ho! A pirate's life for me."

Immediately, the ground started to shake with great force, bringing pieces of rock above the entrance to the cave crashing down. In a panic, Billy rushed to the front of the cave, but heavy dirt and rock was landing all around him. He was trapped and all alone and very afraid, when out of the shadows appeared Monty the Magnificat who reached down and pulled him out of the rocks and dirt to safety.

Minutes seemed like hours as Billy hid underneath a weather-beaten dinghy that had been rotting away on the beach for years. Finally, the earth beneath him began to settle. He stared at the blocked cave entrance. All the secrets he hoped to find inside the cave were lost forever. Monty reached under the dinghy and pulled Billy out and to his feet.

"I don't know what I would do without you, Monty."

"We're friends now, Billy. And friends look out for each other."

As swift as an eagle takes to flight, Monty scaled the side of the mountain and stood on his hind legs at the very top. With his green piercing eyes gazing down below, he let out a tremendous roar that shook the beach. The power of Monty's roar forced Billy backward, and he stumbled and tripped over something sticking out of the ground. Once again, he dug his hands into the ground, this time pulling out an old wine bottle covered in clay beneath the sand. As he brushed away the dried clay, he could see that something was inside. Somehow, he knew what he had just found by the water's edge was a significant part of the puzzle. He wrapped the bottle in an old remnant of a ship's sail he found under the dinghy and made a mad dash back through the same streets where Captain Jack and Mock once traveled. Billy came crashing through the front door, frantic and out of breath. "Dad! Where are you? I found something down at the beach. Hurry!"

"What have you got there, son?" Joe asked, surprised.

"It's an old wine bottle I found on the beach."

Joe held the bottle under the hallway lamp and turned it back and forth. "Well, if I didn't see it for myself, I would not have believed it."

"What is it?"

"It's a message, son, a message in a bottle. Many sailors who were shipwrecked off nearby islands would put a letter inside a bottle to be left to float along the ocean current, with the hope that one day it would be found, and they would be rescued," his father explained.

"Oh boy! I found, a secret message!"

"Well, there's only one way to find out. This bottle is very old and the paper inside is delicate. I must be careful not to destroy the scroll."

"What's a scroll?"

"Well, a scroll is a very thin parchment paper made from calfskin, sheepskin, or goatskin that was used to write

messages or keep records back in ancient times."

Billy watched as his father took a pair of tweezers and carefully pulled the scroll out of the bottle.

"There seems to be a part of the scroll missing and the message is unclear." Joe reached for the magnifying glass and read aloud the words that were carefully etched into the delicate parchment. Tears started to roll down his cheeks. "All men are created equal and no one has the right to deny our God-given right to freedom. In God We Trust, Captain Jack, alias The Hawk."

***

As Billy let out a deep sigh, a cold burst of wind blew the front door wide open and a trail of wet footprints was visible all the way down the hall. The smell of salty sea air grew stronger as they followed the footsteps into the library.

A tall figure of a seafaring pirate, with a sword in his scabbard and boots made of leather, stood pointing at the portrait hanging above the fireplace.

"Oh boy! It's a pirate! A real pirate and he needs our help."

"It's Jon Masterson. He's trying to tell us something."

Joe and his son watched the wall open as if it were summoned by its master and then without warning, the swashbuckling pirate vanished into the cold dark tunnel.

"You know, according to court documents there are a number of slaves missing from the list on the town ledger."

"Dad, we have to find them."

"My son, I believe Captain Jack left this message behind for us to learn the truth and to complete his important work. We must go back into the tunnels and find the answers. Are you with me?"

Billy realized the true meaning of his family heritage and replied, "Aye, aye, Captain."

"I think we'll cover more ground if we split up and search on our own. I don't know how much ground I can cover with this bum hip. So, I'm depending on you, Billy."

Billy proudly grabbed the extra flashlight and began his journey deep into one of the tunnels. He and his father signaled back and forth by tapping on the tunnel wall as they searched for any evidence leading to the forgotten slaves. As Joe walked farther into the tunnel, he noticed his son's tapping begin to fade until it came to an abrupt stop.

Joe continued until he reached the halfway point, but then he had to stop. The pain in his hip was increasing with every step and he had no other choice but to go back and wait for Billy to return.

Deeper into the darkness, Billy thought he heard voices coming from behind the tunnel walls. The more he walked ahead, the louder the voices became. He felt alone and scared. Out of fear, he began to yell out to his father, but all he could hear were the voices getting closer and closer.

The hairs on the back of his neck stood up as a cold rush of air brushed against his cheek. It was as if someone had rushed by him trying to get away from something. As soon as Billy started to run, mysterious ghost-like shadows came creeping out of the walls around him. He stopped dead in his tracks.

"Who are you?" he said in a trembling voice.

The shadows began to cry, "Save our souls!"

The fear Billy felt vanished at the sight of all the forgotten souls left behind centuries before. The clank of shackles coming from the crowd of ghostly phantoms caught his attention. Captain Jack's trusty mate Mock and his feline companion Montego were standing there, just as they were described in the manifest, and pointing toward a gaping hole inside the tunnel wall. Billy slowly reached in and thought he felt something at the tips of his fingers. Encouraged, he stretched as far as he could until he was able to pull out a soiled brown leather pouch.

A powerful rush of wind exploded through the tunnel and pinned Billy against the wall. All he could do was watch as the ghostly phantoms slithered all around him until they disappeared into the cracks within the walls that held him hostage. Suddenly, the razor-sharp sounds of the phantom voices stopped, and Billy fell to the ground. He called out to his father for help, but all he could hear was the sound of his own heartbeat echoing throughout the cave. Minutes became hours as he crawled along the wet and slimy floor of Captain Jack's underground refuge. Everywhere he turned, ghostly shadows swirled in and out of the walls around him. He was very weary and about to lose consciousness when he thought he heard a voice in the distance calling out to him.

"Come with me, Billy. I will show you the way," the mysterious voice said.

The pitch-black darkness blinded him from seeing who or what grabbed his hand, but for some strange reason he felt safe and unafraid. The rattling of chains behind him faded away as he moved closer to the end of his journey. A sigh of relief came over him as he heard his father calling out to him.

"Billy? Billy? Can you hear me? Where are you?"

Billy turned to look back and was stunned by the sight of Captain Jack McDevitt standing just a few feet away and looking as real as the nose on his face. This time, he felt no need to cover his eyes from fear and watched as Captain Jack's spirit faded away.

"Did you see him, Dad? Did you see Captain Jack?"

"I'm sorry, son. I didn't see anyone, but I can feel his presence all around us. What happened back in the tunnel?"

"It's a long story, Dad, but I have something for you to see."

"We better get back. It's getting late and the pain is getting much worse."

Billy helped his father back to the house and gave him the last of his pain medicine. Within the hour, his father was ready to see what Billy had found in the tunnel wall.

"What have you got there? Let's see what's inside."

Once again, Billy watched as his father gently removed another scroll and placed it on the vintage desk. He pulled out a wooden box inside the desk drawer and compared the scrolls side by side.

"What does it say, Pop?"

"This is it! It's the last known list of runaway slaves left behind by Captain Jack and Mock, all those centuries ago. So, what happened back there in the tunnel? I was beginning to get worried."

"I heard voices and the ghosts were flying all around me, and then Captain Jack pointed to the secret place inside the wall, and I reached in and found the pouch, but I couldn't find my way out and somebody grabbed my hand and..."

"Slow down Billy. You're safe now. Let's put the scroll in a safe place, because tomorrow is going to be a very important day for our family."

Early the next morning, they proudly gathered the pieces of their family history and set out to meet with a visiting member from the South Carolina Historical Society, who was to arrive that morning.

"C'mon, Pop. We're going to be late."

"I need you to drive, son."

In order to save time, Joe and Billy headed down the back trails once used by early settlers and met up with Michael and Timmy outside the entrance to the Chamber of Commerce.

"The meeting is about to begin. Let's get inside," Michael suggested.

In a unanimous vote, the Society members agreed to add the remaining names to complete the official registry of slaves who went missing during the underground movement.

"The Historical Society will be proud to display the names of all those who labored on this land," Robert Brock announced.

"Thank you for helping my dad, Mr. Brock."

"You're quite welcome, Billy, but you better get your father home. He needs to get his rest."

"Well, Joe," said Michael, Billy found the last remaining link to one man whose vision to make a difference will inspire future generations to recognize that we are all created equal."

"Will Captain Jack and all the slaves be safe now?" Billy asked.

"Son, you single-handedly brought Captain Jack and all the slaves back to the one place they can truly call home.

Michael, do you know anyone that could help me search the rest of the tunnels under my house?"

"I think I know of two young men who have earned the title of quartermaster."

The boys jumped with excitement and took off running down the cobblestone streets of their seafaring town.

"Hey, Billy! You have to tell me everything that happened in the tunnel with Captain Jack."

"How about I show you instead?" he replied as they stumbled into the private library.

As they stood out of breath in front of the entrance to the tunnels, the boys raised their fists in the air and began shouting in true pirate form.

"Yo! Ho! Yo! Ho! A pirates' life for me. A pirate's life for me. A pirate's life for me!"

THE END.

Don't miss out!

Visit the website below and you can sign up to receive emails whenever Tina Haydamacha publishes a new book. There's no charge and no obligation.

https://books2read.com/r/B-A-PAPI-DWZZ

BOOKS2READ

Connecting independent readers to independent writers.

About the Author

Tina Haydamacha, a wife, mother and passionate writer is a former graduate of The Charles Morris Price School for Advertising and Journalism. Her passion for writing began as a young child waking up in the middle of the night to write her thoughts down on any paper she could find. The gravitational pull to write a story was always a dream, until one day during the pursuit of another passion within the science field, her English professor presented an opportunity to interpret Edward Albee's, The American Dream. The arduous challenge put her writing to the test and by completion validated her love for the craft. Soon after, she was recognized by her professor, who made her critique of The American Dream available to all students as a reference guide in the college library. This experience reignited her passion for writing and led her to write a screenplay about the CIA takeover of Saturday Morning Cartoons now residing in the Writer's Guild East. Growing up surrounded by an artistic family gave her the platform to begin her journey in writing, hoping one day to become a published author. The idea of bringing characters to life in a story she created led her to publish her first ebook "Monty the Magnificat" in 2019. Her story continues with her second book "Teddy & The Mighty YOLO" soon to be manuscript ready.

facebook.com/tinahaydamacha.author

https://www.storyrocket.com/Tina.3eb48518
https://www.instagram.com/tinahaydamacha
https://tinytealeaf.wixsite.com/mysite

Read more at https://www.storyrocket.com/monty-the-magnificat.

www.ingramcontent.com/pod-product-compliance
Lightning Source LLC
Chambersburg PA
CBHW031742150726
47989CB00006B/2566